DISCARDED
THE
UNIVERSITY OF WINNIPEG
PORTAGE & BALMORAL
WINNIPEG, MAN.
CANADA

The Aristocrats

The Aristocrats

Being the impressions of the *Lady*
HELEN POLE during her sojourn
in The Great North Woods
as spontaneously recorded in
her *letters* to her friend
in North Britain the
Countess of EDGE
and ROSS

By GERTRUDE ATHERTON

THE GREGG PRESS / RIDGEWOOD, N. J.

First published in 1901 by John Lane
Republished in 1968 by
The Gregg Press Incorporated
171 East Ridgewood Avenue
Ridgewood, New Jersey, U.S.A.

Library of Congress Catalog Card Number: 68-20003

Printed in the United States of America

AMERICANS IN FICTION

In the domain of literature the play may once have been the chief abstract and chronicle of the times, but during the nineteenth and twentieth centuries the novel has usurped the chief place in holding the mirror up to the homely face of society. On this account, if for no other, the Gregg Press series of reprints of American fiction merits the attention of all students of Americana and of librarians interested in building up adequate collections dealing with the social and literary history of the United States. Most of the three score and ten novels or volumes of short stories included in the series enjoyed considerable fame in their day but have been so long out of print as to be virtually unobtainable in the original editions.

Included in the list are works by writers not presently fashionable in critical circles—but nevertheless well known to literary historians—among them Joel Chandler Harris, Harriet Beecher Stowe, Thomas Bailey Aldrich, and William Gilmore Simms. A substantial element in the list consists of authors who are known especially for their graphic portrayal of a particular American setting, such as Gertrude Atherton (California), Arlo Bates (Boston), Alice Brown (New England), Edward Eggleston (Indiana), Mary Wilkins Freeman (New England), Henry B. Fuller (Chicago), Richard M. Johnston (Georgia), James Lane Allen (Kentucky), Mary N. Murfree (Tennessee), and Thomas Nelson Page (Virginia). There is even a novel by Frederic Remington, one of the most popular painters of the Western cowboy and Indian—and another, and impressive minor classic on the early mining region of Colorado, from the pen of Mary Hallock Foote. The professional student of American literature will rejoice in the opportunity afforded by the collection to extend his reading of fiction belonging to what is called the "local-color movement"—a major current in the development of the national belles-lettres.

Among the titles in the series are also a number of famous historical novels. Silas Weir Mitchell's *Hugh Wynne* is one of the very best fictional treatments of the American Revolution. John Esten Cooke is the foremost Southern writer of his day who dealt with the Civil War. The two books by Thomas Dixon are among the most famous novels on the Reconstruction Era, with sensational disclosures of the original Ku Klux Klan in action. They supplied the grist for the first great movie "spectacular"—*The Birth of a Nation* (1915).

Paul Leicester Ford's *The Honorable Peter Stirling* is justly ranked among the top American novels which portray American politics in action—a subject illuminated by other novelists in the Gregg list—A. H. Lewis, Frances H. Burnett, and Alice Brown, for example. Economic problems are forcefully put before the reader in works by Aldrich, Mrs. Freeman, and John Hay, whose novels illustrate the ominous concern over the early battles between labor and capital. From the sweatshops of Eastern cities in which newly arrived immigrants toiled for pittances, to the Western mining camps where the laborers packed revolvers, the working class of the times enters into various other stories in the Gregg list. The capitalist class, also, comes in for attention, with an account of a struggle for the ownership of a railroad in Samuel Merwin's *The Short-Line War* and with the devastating documentation of the foibles of the newly rich and their wives in the narratives of David Graham Phillips. It was Phillips whose annoying talent for the exposure of abuses led Theodore Roosevelt to put the term "muck-raker" into currency.

While it is apparent that local-color stories, the historical novel, and the economic novel have all been borne in mind in choosing the titles for this important series of reprints, it is evident that careful consideration has also been given to treatments of various minority elements in the American population. The Negro, especially, but also the Indian, the half-breed, Creoles, Cajuns—and even the West Coast Japanese—appear as characters in various of these novels or volumes of short stories and sketches. Joel Chandler Harris's *Free Joe* will open the eyes of readers who know that author solely as the creator of humorous old Uncle Remus. And there is a revelatory volume of dialect tales, written by a Negro author, *The Conjure Woman* by Charles W. Chesnutt.

In literary conventions and the dominating attitudes toward life, the works in the Gregg series range from the adventurous romance illustrated so well by Mayne Reid or the polite urbanity of Owen Wister to the mordant irony of Kate Chopin and the grimmer realism of Joseph Kirkland's own experiences on bloody Civil War battlefields or the depressing display of New York farm life by Harold Frederic. In short, the series admirably illustrates the general qualities of the fiction produced in the United States during the era covered, just as it generously mirrors the geographical regions, the people, and the problems of the times.

PROFESSOR CLARENCE GOHDES
Duke University
Durham, North Carolina

December, 1967

GERTRUDE ATHERTON

Gertrude Atherton was born in San Francisco in 1857, and died in 1948. Her father was Thomas Lodowick Horn, who came to California in the 1850's, and her mother was also an early settler. Mrs. Atherton was educated at several private schools, the last being Sayre Institute in Lexington, Kentucky. In 1876 she married George Henry Bowen Atherton, and they lived in Fair Oaks, California (now called Atherton). Mrs. Atherton began to write while still a schoolgirl. Soon after her marriage she published a short novel in the San Francisco *Argonaut,* and wrote her first full-length novel, *What Dreams May Come.* She went to New York in the 1880's after the death of her husband. In World War I, she did relief work in France, and received the Legion of Honor. *The Conqueror* (1902) is her most popular novel, though perhaps not her best work, and sold over a half million copies. Mrs. Atherton was inspired by California life, especially the influence of the Spanish "before the gringo came," but she also wrote stories about American life in other localities and periods, such as *Senator North,* an important novel of Washington politics which also deals with the "Negro problem." She has been unjustly criticized as being merely a writer of "light fiction," but in fact her works frequently attack the vital social dilemmas that concerned American society in the nineteenth century, particularly the impact of the aggressive, hard-working Yankee upon more polished, indolent cultures. Her novels show both a direct knowledge of American society and the results of serious and detailed historical research. She is a first-rate storyteller — hence her popular appeal — and her novels and stories move swiftly and smoothly, without digressions or didactic passages.

F. C. S.

To

All Lovers
of
The ADIRONDACK *Peaks*
and *Forests* and *Lakes*
this little volume
is dedicated
By
An Alien but Ardent and
Grateful Admirer
H. P.

Letter I

FROM *the Lady* HELEN POLE *to the Countess of* EDGE *and* ROSS.

Boulder Lake, THE GREAT NORTH WOODS, Hamilton County, New York, U. S. A.

June 16th

Dear Polly

AM on top of a mountain by a lake, with other mountains towering irregularly in all directions; a primeval wilderness, in fact, for every mountain is covered with a dense forest, and we reached our lake by an ascent up an almost perpendicular "corduroy" road—made of logs. Agatha and I walked most of the time, for the way the horses stumbled and strained was appalling. Of course poor Bertie had to stay in the "buckboard"—a sort of box on wheels without springs—and stand the terrible jolting; but I think the unique experience diverted him and he would have enjoyed it rather if it had not been for the poor horses. I could not look at them, and lingered some distance behind and stared into this wonderful forest. The Adirondacks are said to be one of the original ranges of the earth, and when one reflects that these spruces and maples and hemlocks and birches had great-grandfathers about the same time—the sensation is almost uncanny, and I realise how overcivilised we all are. Not that I am blasée at twenty-six. God forbid; and I never have been so keen about anything in my life as I am to see every rapidly succeeding phase of this extraordinary country. It is so new, so various, so contradictory, so vital, so un-European.

But to return to the Adirondacks. By the merest good fortune we did not have to go to an hotel, for, in spite of the fact that we brought over a retinue of servants, I am sure that even Quick never would have known how to go to work to find a house in this wilderness, and it would have come to our taking a floor—if we could get it—of some hotel, and having no end of bother. But on the Oceanic we got to know rather well a Mr. Rogers, who belongs to one of the many clubs that own lakes and tracts in the Adirondacks, and he offered us his house or "camp"—said that his mother and sister were going abroad this summer, and that he could live at the Club House, which he preferred. Of course Bertie and Agatha demurred, as the club rules would not permit Mr. Rogers to accept any rent; but I said at once to take it, and gave them no peace till they consented. I urged that we could repay Mr. Rogers' hospitality a hundred fold in England, that we all hated hotels and bother, and that it was of the utmost importance to settle Bertie at once. Now they are very grateful to me, for Bertie, poor darling, is better already, and the house is not only comfortable but charming. It would hold five or six people besides the servants, and is built of big logs, with the rough bark on, and an upper and lower veranda connected by little flights of stairs. Inside it is "sealed" with diagonal strips of polished wood instead of plaster; the floors are also of hard wood with rugs, and the furniture is mostly cane and very picturesque and jolly. In the living room is a huge fireplace of stones with the moss on, the low ceiling is crossed with heavy beams, and there are several mounted deer-heads. From the front verandas and windows we get a fine view of the lake and the little irregularities which form its bays, but on all other sides we look directly into the forest. There is no clearing to speak of about the house, and the tall spruce trees, pointed like church spires, and the maples with their delicate beautiful leaves form a perfect wall; for their branches grow to the very ground. It is all very wild, and I am writing to you on a table made from the lower section and part of the roots of a tree.

But I must tell you of something that happened on the journey. It interested me deeply. We did not make the journey too comfortably. Agatha sent all the servants but Bertie's man, Parker, and including our maids, to the lake three days before ourselves, in order that our unconscionable number of boxes might be unpacked, and the place look as familiar to Bertie as possible. At New York and Albany we did not miss the servants and took for granted that wherever there were shillings there were porters. But at a city with a Greek name, where we had to change cars, we found ourselves standing on the platform in the midst of portmanteaux, and Parker with his hands full supporting Bertie, who was terribly knocked up by the trip. I asked a man if there were no porters, and he said, "nup." I forgot to say that poor Agatha had one of her headaches, and for once everything devolved upon me. She sank down upon a bench and looked as if she never intended to move again. Parker assisted Bertie into the waiting-room, and then went in search of tea and rolls. I approached a policeman. He was a big manly looking fellow, and I was sure he would help me. He did, the dear thing. When I asked him to tell me where I could find a porter, he said, "No porters here, but I'll take your things to the parcel room. Your train won't be along for forty-five minutes." At the parcel window, when he had handed all those big portmanteaux in and got me a cheque, I offered him a quarter of a dollar, about the equivalent of our shilling. He refused it so nicely. "Another time," he said. I apologized, saying that the act was mechanical, and he smiled and said, "Well, I guess you'll find that we can help a lady for nothing up here." He then pointed out the restaurant at the end of the platform, and after I had assisted Agatha there, and had a cup of the most shocking tea I ever tasted, I looked him up again; for I was so much interested in his refusal to accept a tip that I wanted to talk to him. Agatha had subsided beside Bertie, and would not have cared if I had stood on my head on the platform. I began by asking him if he would help us on to the train, and he said emphatically that he would, and then we talked about tipping, and both agreed that it was a pernicious system, calculated to destroy a man's self-respect. He added with a fine scorn that he did not see how a man who thought anything of himself could take any money but his wages, particularly from a lady. Then he asked me if I wasn't English, and if my brother—or husband?—"brother, I guess, you don't look married"—were not consumptive. "He looks it," he added; "but not too far gone for the Adirondacks to set him up." And then we talked about the cheerful subject of consumption, and he seemed quite pleased when I told him that so far Bertie had not developed tuberculosis, although he had had twenty-six hemorrhages in the last two years, and was getting weaker all the time. He told me I mustn't worry, but give him all the mountain air he could swallow and all the sunshine he could "soak in." I couldn't make the man out at all. He had the monumental dignity of our policemen, but he talked to me exactly as if I were his equal, and, as he had no thought of taking a liberty, with no offensive familiarity. And yet he certainly was not a gentleman working for his living; just a plain, ordinary—well, I suppose the word American will do as well as any other. All the Americans I have met think a jolly lot of themselves, and I suppose my policeman was one of the finer flowers of the Declaration of Independence. After he had helped us into the train he shook hands with me and said he'd look forward to seeing me again on my way back. "I knew you were English the moment I set eyes on you," he said, "and I thought by your looks you were very proud, and high-and-mighty, but the minute you spoke I seen you were just as nice as nice could be, and I'm glad to have done what I could for you." As the train moved out of the station I bowed to him and he touched his helmet with his club like an officer saluting. Now what do *you* make of him?

There's not a soul up here yet but ourselves; so you'll doubtless be inflicted with another letter in a day or two. I must go and read to Bertie. He is swinging in a hammock on the front veranda in the sun and *does* seem so much better. The mornings and nights are cold, but for several hours during the day the sun is heavenly, and one feels so close to it up here. You, too, are a lone figure, not on a mountain but on a moor, and dreadfully *ennuyée*, I fear; so relieve your loneliness after my fashion and write to me often. I know that you have someone else to write to—alas! that I have not—but heaven knows you must have time for us both. What a thousand pities Freddy could not have died a glorious death rescuing some one from the lions when they were walking the streets of Umtali, or trying to assassinate Mr. Kruger. I am not blood-thirsty, but we all have to die some time, and Freddy *is* so wicked, and has made you so unhappy, and there *is* such a chance of happiness for you, and I do so hate to think of you in a divorce court with all the world reading the hateful particulars. Well, it is all on the knees of the gods.

Bertie sends you his love, and I send you all of mine you have not already.

HELEN.

Letter II

From the Lady HELEN POLE *to the Countess of* EDGE *and* ROSS.

Boulder Lake,
June 18th

I WISH you were up here with me, Polly; I am sure you would forget all your troubles. It is such an extraordinary experience to be in a primeval wilderness, where one never hears a church bell, never comes suddenly upon a wayside calvary, never passes a peasant in costume, nor a picturesque hovel. The civilisations and the arts that have made Europe such an inexhaustible wonder never have ventured here. It is Nature, virgin and ignorant, and it often gives me the most unaccountable sensation. Perhaps when I am more familiar with it, I shall be more successful in defining it. I have not grasped the spirit of the place yet. There is nothing of the frowning majestic awesomeness of wild mountain regions that I have read of and often imagined, and, as surely, there is nothing of the peace of England—that peace that must pervade any perfected civilisation just as repose comes to the truly cultivated mind of middle years. It is something between the two, beauty without tameness, solitude without calm, yet with none of the feverish restlessness of the young civilisation at its feet, primeval wildness without its terrors; for scarcely a living thing that harms, human or brute, but has been exterminated; noble heights that never frown. There you have the Adirondacks as I am able to interpret them to you at present. They give me an intense pleasure, that is all I can add. As we approached the mountains on the day of our arrival I thought I should be disappointed, the foliage looked so *soft*. From a distance one could not define a single tree; they are so densely limbed and leafed, their branches grow so low, and they crowd so closely, that the mountains looked as if covered by a thick shrubbery, through which a path never had been cut, and out of which not a tree projected. But after we were in the mountains all was changed, we drove through the very heart of the woods, thick with high trees and full of a pleasant gloom; and once in approaching them we passed a hill that looked to be set close with green church spires, so thick were the spruce among the maples.

The trees about the lake grow down to the edge of the brown water, almost out of it, and so densely, that in rowing past, one rarely has a glimpse into the woods. When one does, it is to see the great boulders that have given the lake its name. They, too, are on the edge of the lake, covered with moss that sometimes is green, sometimes a mingling of the most delicate tints, pink and green and pearl and blue. Rioting everywhere along the edge of the lake is the wild honeysuckle, pink and intoxicatingly fragrant. By the Club House is an open field where they raise hay. Just now it looks like a wild lawn full of buttercups and daisies, almost as much of an anomaly up here in this wilderness as these comfortable houses and gayly painted boats.

And the perfumes and the silence! how can I describe them? The fresh primitive smell of earth that never has been turned, the sensuous sweetness of the honeysuckle, the strong resinous vitalising odour of the balsam tree. And the silence just misses being oppressive. The birds sing one at a time. I have not yet heard a duet, much less a chorus. Once in a while, there is the tinkle of a cow-bell, and the wind is always playing gently with the tree-tops.

For a few days I greatly feared that Bertie would hate it, but he lies for hours in the hammock, a balsam pillow beside him, either sleeping or listening while Agatha or I read to him. He vows that he will shoot deer with Mr. Rogers in September. That gives him two months and a half —I wonder! I think I should be so happy I should quite go off my head. But he is so young, and only a few of our ancestors have died of consumption. Agatha, dear old mother, is conscious-stricken, because the disease did not attack her instead of Bertie, and, although she never would admit it, I think my aggressive health annoys her. I believe that if I had rosy cheeks she would have left me behind; but if I am white instead of pink, I have the deep vitality that I know Bertie ought to have. I expect he often wonders, poor darling, why his sisters of forty and six-and-twenty should have long superfluous lives before them, while he, at barely eight and twenty, is stricken and miserable. Agatha says it is the will of God, but I am afraid it was going the pace and wet feet. Agatha frowns sternly when I suggest that it was more Bertie's fault than the Almighty's, for although she will admit that wet feet might have something to do with it, she will not even listen to a hint of Bertie's well-known delinquencies, will not admit, dear austere nun-like soul, that such things exist in the world. She is still inexorably opposed to your divorce, Polly; says that it is the duty of a wife to accept her fate, etc., and when I try to explain, she tells me I have no right to know anything about such shocking things that do not really exist (God save her blessed inconsistent soul), and walks austerely out of the room.

But we do know things, don't we, Polly? I wonder if, in face of all I have been so close to, I ever shall have the temerity to enter the undemonstratable state of matrimony? Of course I know of a decent number of comfortable marriages, and—well, two—happy ones, but somehow the others, particularly yours, stand out; to say nothing of the fact that all the girls who married in our first season, eight long years ago, are flashing pretty strong. Sometimes I feel like a widow with a past! But how many confidences I have listened to, and how much sympathy I have been called upon to pour into temporarily blighted lives! It is a blessed relief to be here in this silence and fragrance and beauty; and when the horrors that men and women make for themselves come into my mind, I go out and look at the solitary peak that towers above the long receding range of mountains at the head of the lake. Sometimes it is pale blue, sometimes light green; under a rain storm it is a lurid grey. More often there are long shadows on it, which constantly change in form, and the highest wind never seems to ruffle its forests. It takes the significance out of our petty civilisation and I sometimes wish I could live alone on it. I don't suppose I really do, though. Of course I have not lived yet, myself, and I dream my dreams, and hope for better things than I have seen. I have filled my writing-desk with balsam and I hope a little of its healthy fragrance may reach you.

19th

To-day I had an experience which, in a way, reminded me of my policeman. Once or twice I had noticed about the house a stout straight freckled-faced girl, a daughter of a villager on an outer spur of the mountains who was pressed into service by our invaluable Quick when the house-maid he engaged in New York deserted him in the earlier stages of the journey. As I came out of the woods this morning our rural hand-maiden marched up to me with an almost defiant air, a very high colour, and said:

"I'd like to speak to a dook, ma'am, I mean lady."

"Really?" I said.

"Yes, I'm going away. It's the first place I've ever lived in where the hired girls didn't eat with the family, and I haven't felt nice since I've bin here. I don't see any reason why you should be so terrible proud if you are English; and all the help sayin' 'your grace' and 'your ladyship,' makes my flesh crawl."

"We are not proud," I began, but she interrupted me passionately.

"Oh, yes you are. You hold your head as if the ground warn't good enough for you to walk on. I can't help lookin' at you because you're so beautiful with your black hair and your blue eyes and white skin, and your nose is just lovely! That there Lady Agatha don't look so very different from any other old maid that I can see, and I'm sure she dresses wors'n anything I *ever* seen. I don't mind her, but *you—you*—make me feel like dirt. I just stare and stare at you and hate myself because I can't keep from wishin' I was you——" Here she made a struggle to control her voice and keep down her tears. "I went to school till a year ago," she continued, "and I've paid lots of visits to well-to-do farmers in this county, whose daughters has had a year's schoolin' in Utica, and I call them all by their first names—so I can't bear to feel the way you and all these high-toned help make me feel——"

Here I felt so sorry for her, she was so plainly suffering in her dumb lacerated pride, that I took her hand and patted it. "Don't worry about all that," I said. "We belong to different countries, that is all. Everything is on quite another plan in England. I can imagine how absurd our old-fashioned titles must seem to you over here. You see how wise your ancestors were to drop them. I cannot help mine, but I can assure you that I am not proud—I never have thought of such a thing. It is you who are proud, and I think your pride very fine. Why do you wish to see my brother?"

She was somewhat mollified by this time and answered with a flash of anticipation in her eyes:

"Because I've read about dooks and I'd give my eyes to speak to one. I didn't kinder believe there were such things outside of books and noospapers."

"Well, you shall speak to my brother," I said. "Come with me." I led the way to the veranda, not without misgivings, for I did not know what sort of humour our invalid would be in. And he *was* in a wax about something.

"Bertie," I said, "here is a young person, native

to this beautiful wilderness, who wants to speak to you, being under the delusion that Dukes are quite unlike ordinary mortals."

Bertie, who was muffled up in a horrid old overcoat, with white mits on his hands, glowered over his book.

"What rot!" he exclaimed. "What infernal rot. I should think you would have more sense. I wish you'd get me a decent novel. I hate these American things—all analysis, epigrams, scenery and virtue. America must be a provincial hole. Fetch me——"

But I had hastened the maiden away. As she was about to retire to the back regions, she stopped and turned her head.

"Well," she remarked, "I guess I'm as good as he is, anyway. White mits! My land! *He* don't make me feel nobody, only tired." And she looked quite pleased as she flirted her skirts through the doorway.

This letter should go by parcel post!

My love to you.

HELEN.

Letter III

From the Lady HELEN POLE *to the Countess of* EDGE *and* ROSS.

Boulder Lake,
June 23d

Dearest Poll:

NONE of the Club people here yet, and if it were not for newspapers and letters—a man in the employ of the Club climbs this perpendicular mountain every evening with the post—I should cease to believe in a world which lives in my mind as a mere clash of sound. It *is* so quiet here! Sometimes when I am alone in my room I throw a shawl over the clock to muffle its ticking. It seems a cheap intrusion upon this colossal silence. I have been in the woods for hours at a time when not even a bird has trilled, nothing but that soft soughing of the unsleeping wind in the tree-tops. In the evening an occasional caw-caw comes from the forest, a lonesome cricket shrills, a frog croaks in the reeds.

I often go deep down into the forest and listen to the faint monotonous hum of the leaves, always a soft sound, when one gets away from the rigid spruce, because the leaves of the maple are as delicate in texture as they are in tint. And these leaves, in places, seem to fill the woods. Unless you throw back your head you barely realise the existence of the trees, only that gently moving lace-like curtain of green many-pointed leaves that meets the leafy ground. The sunlight splashes here and there. I have found a gorge whose gloom is eternal; in the friendlier depths the twilight is almost green. You know how I despise all theologies and churches and vulgar public demonstration of what should be man's most sacred inner life; but when I am alone in the forest I always say my prayers; and that occasional solitary communion with God is surely the only true religion for intelligent beings. I have heard of "revival meetings" in which people "stand up and confess Christ." *Public emotions*. How unutterably vulgar and cheaply sensational. And what pleasure can a religion be that is shared with the multitude, that is formulated, ticketed, branded with the approval of others? I hope everybody I know, except the one or two I love, thinks me a pagan. I am jealous of what is more truly my own than anything else can ever be.

But to return to my woods. I have spoken of the sleepless wind, but occasionally it goes elsewhere, and I have sat for hours on one of the boulders which strew these mountains, born of some unimaginable convulsion, modelled by unrecorded glaciers, and waited eagerly for even a bird to give the silence a tiny but startling shake. And yet, as I have written you before, I think, there is none of the peace of England here. But it is magnificent, this feeling of lofty remoteness, of standing just under the sky, of feeling and hearing the silence. There is sweetness and charm rather than grandeur in these woods, but still not peace. Nature is much like human nature. While her youth lasts—and how much man has to do with the quickening of time!—she suggests turbulence in her silences, there is something disquieting, even forbidding, in that very sweetness which is a careless incidental gift. Sometimes when I am alone in the forest, a mile or more from home, not even another "trail" but the one I dare not leave, the ferns and dogwood brushing my waist, that broken green curtain motionless against a colossal boulder, not a sound, not a fleeting suggestion of any world beyond those ancient trees with their young leaves, those immeasurable depths with other mountains and other forests beyond them, all beauty, the very idealisation of one's dreams of the "forest primeval," the isolation of mountain-tops made manifest, a fear comes over me which I have no more been able to define than I have yielded to. I know that the bear is infrequent and harmless, the panther is gone for ever, that a poisonous snake has never been seen on the Adirondacks, that tramps are unheard of, and that I cannot lose my way if I keep to the trail. And as you know I am what is called heroic, and have spent hours alone on English moors and in English woods. Never before have I felt the sudden terror that assails me here in this beautiful gentle and unthinkably aged forest, with its eternal virginal youth. Some day the meaning of it will come to me suddenly, like the girl's face in the moon; you know I manage to get to the core of most things.

Bertie is getting a little bored, and is restless,

but is so much better that he is very good-natured about it. He takes a short walk with me in the forest every day, and a row when the sun is full on the lake. I often row him, it is so good to have him all to myself. Agatha has been the best of mothers to us, but after all she is *not* our mother, and she is almost too old for a sister. We love her, but we love each other far more, more indeed than we ever have loved anyone else, but Dad; and sometimes when in his wretched physical weakness Bertie drops his head on my shoulder, and becomes as confidential with me as in his innocent boy days, I see into a soul that has more good in it than bad, and much strength in spite of the sad weakness his broken confessions reveal. I am sure now that if he recovers he will become as useful, if not as great, a man as Dad. Ah, there was a man! He admired Agatha from a distance, but he kept us two so close to him that we ought to be a thousand times better and more sensible than we are. But he has been dead six long years, Bertie has rank and riches, and I am beautiful. What hope that the world would let us alone!

Agatha is so happy at Bertie's improvement that she does not care—except on his account—whether the lake people come up at all or not, and, besides, she is too good to be bored. I do not mean that sarcastically, for these people who are constantly thinking of others never have time to sit down and commiserate their Ego.

This evening I was down at the edge of the lake watching the sunset—a blue one of many shades, from limpid pale blue lakes to masses of rich ultramarine, instead of the usual splendour of red and gold—when the keeper passed me in a boat. He paused and pointed to the end of the lake.

"Fog's goin' up the mountain, Miss," he said. "Sure sign of rain; and I heard a cuckoo in the woods to-day, another sign as never fails. I guess them big fireplaces 'll come in handy for a day or two." Fortunately we have plenty to read.

I forgot to tell you that Jemima, our erstwhile handmaiden, of whom I wrote you, and who is now "visiting" the lake-keeper's family, yesterday brought me two charming offerings, a basket of wild strawberries from the meadow and a bunch of half-wild half-cultivated pink roses. I simply buried my face in the roses, their sweetness was so poignant, so delicious, that I wanted to inhale and absorb it all at once, and I pressed them to every bit of my face and neck. The strawberries, too, were so fragrant! such tiny things, but with a most agreeable acid sweetness. I have not seen Bertie enjoy anything so much for a long time; and when I could no longer smell my roses—alas! for the quick blunting of mortal sense!—I smothered Bertie's face in their pink fragrance and enjoyed them again, vicariously.

24th

I received your first long letter last night and I have read it no less than four times. That proves a good many things, does it not?—that you write the most interesting letters in the world, that I am interested in all that concerns you, and that I have no other correspondent. Freddy certainly is amusing; there is a touch of farce in every tragedy; but I am glad you have not answered his effusions even sarcastically. And I am glad the days of duelling are over. It is true that V. R. would settle the whole question promptly, but then there would be a scandal, which has been avoided so far, and still can be, even with the inevitable divorce. But I know how hard it all is on you, and fancy-free as I am and always have been, I can well imagine that the separation is the hardest of all.

I am hoping my letters cheer and interest you. It is all so interesting to me, here in this wilderness of the new world—I feel exactly like one of the old colonials—that I love to write about it.

It has been storming for a week, cold and wind and rain; and we have spent the time in the living-room, about the big rock fireplace filled with blazing logs. We are very cosy within, and have plenty to read, and Bertie says he likes it for a change; but I never heard such howling furious winds. Every now and again there is a crash in the forest and I run to the window. But that wall of trees, with its branches to the ground, is impenetrable. It creaks and bends and grinds, and the beeches and maples shake wildly in the blast, but there is no rift. But I can imagine the wild scene, the ruin in those forest depths. What isolation! And how like the storms that rage in our inner life that no mortal eye ever glimpses. My woods suggest virgin sweetness no longer. That wall of wet angry leaves surrounding a blind furious struggle of forces, the writhing fighting trees raging at being assaulted by the elements, shrieking through the forest when they are overcome, the torn surface of the lake, all give me a feeling of delicious terror, and I wish that I were a poet.

Bertie, while we were in New York, subscribed for no less than seven newspapers, and Mr. Rogers kindly made me out a list of the best American novels of the past ten years, every one of which I bought. I have read the newspapers aloud to Bertie ever since our arrival, and during this week I have read—to myself; Bertie does his own novel reading,—just twenty-six works of American fiction. After a two week's course of the newspapers I had come to the conclusion that the United States was the most full-blooded nation the world had ever known; bursting with virility and energy, a great lusty young giant, full of good and bad, sophisticated, but so busy as to have retained a certain native ingenuousness; its cities presenting the very extremes of virtue and vice; the monotony of its Western farms varied by picturesque desperadoes;—but I have wandered from my simile: I was trying to say that the young giant was an extraordinary compound of primeval passions, with the force that those passions alone are the mainspring of, and the sophistication which the old world flung into his brain the day his eyes saw the light; a little like a raging lion with the soul of a man. In some of the newspapers these extremes meet; in others I find either the intense conservatism or the rampant radicalism which are bound to be in this country of extremes; but in even an old fogy like the Morning ——* I find the same suggestion, doubtless because young men write for it, although under a restraint that has evidently never been heard of in the offices of the Morning ——.*

But the literature of the country! It would give

* Deletions by the publisher.

one a precisely opposite impression of "Americanism." It is true that in England I had read three or four American novels that seemed to me full of blood and life, but I infer they are not literature, for they are not on Mr. Rogers' list (he inherited, grew up in, one of the three or four distinguished publishing houses of the country, so I suppose he knows), and, judging from these twenty-six novels, I should, had Bertie failed to subscribe for those papers, have concluded that the United States was in about the middle stage of anæmia, not yet in the pernicious stage, but with blood dangerously watered. These books, judging by the extracts from reviews at the back, and the number of editions quoted, have been lauded by the critics, and well patronised by the public—the same public which makes up the component parts of the lusty young giant. I must say I cannot see him reading his literature. It is superlatively well written; frequently it has brilliancy and style and form; the touch of both men and women is, often, almost elusively delicate; the conversations sprightly and epigrammatic; the sentiments most proper and elevated; the side of life shown is almost invariably life as it ought to be, not as it is; nobody's taste is offended, nobody is told anything he ought not to know (he can learn all that every day in the newspapers, some of which claim to have a million readers); they are always readable and seldom commonplace. But they never by any chance forsake the obvious. Altogether, one feels in the most excellent, elegant, irreproachable company, for even in a story of the slums, or one containing, perchance, an irregular baby, the author keeps you close to himself and whispers it all to you; he never lets the objectionable directly offend your sensitive soul. I now am inclined to believe that old story of the drawers on the piano legs, What is the keynote of this American literature? I have hunted for it industriously and talked it over with Bertie. We both have come to the conclusion that it is intended to be "aristocratic." That is the only way in which we can explain the literature of this most strenuous and vigorous of nations. High above the hurly-burly certain of its cultivated members, gifted with a pretty trick of words, are endeavouring to create a rarefied atmosphere which only the elect can enter, where those that do enter prove themselves to be of the elect. Roast beef, roast goose, plum pudding and burgundy, bread and butter and potatoes, apples and Yorkshire pudding are never served; only the entrées, the thin red and white wines that warm gently, but never intoxicate; champagne at rare intervals, and never, Oh, never! in my lady's slipper;—the most dainty and expensive sweets, ice-creams of exceptional make, never common vanilla or chocolate, and occasionally—I should have put it first—a ducky little cutlet; birds, of course, caviare, and—Oh, I had forgotten, no *pie*. Pie is a universal taste, therefore bourgeois, like roast beef. And Bertie and I are so devoted to roast beef, and have formed almost a passion for pie! Bertie says he will lie and count the leaves on the trees before he will read another, and even Agatha says they are unsatisfactory, and that she prefers sermons—occasionally she reads one aloud to us! I never have taken kindly to this form of literature, but I really think, with all their obsolete ideas, they have more substance, more *inside*, than these lively, modern, educational, elegant, but—timid novels. I wonder if that is the word and why? I'll ask Mr. Rogers.

Two or three of the newspapers, as I told you, are stately and conservative, and I notice that their review columns have the exact tone of the literature. I was told in New York that their sales were small but intensely aristocratic — so much so that a popular politician could not afford to be seen with one—and that the sensational papers had enormous circulations, and were by no means ignored by "the very best people," that they did good by exposing the "crooked" methods of monopolists and all sorts of abuses, and that they wielded an immense political influence —also that many of the creators of the nation's bloodless masterpieces wrote occasionally for them —for a high consideration—and were not averse from reaching the larger audience. It now comes back to me, I once heard that there is an immense sale in the United States for the sort of literature forbidden by our County Council. Yet there is no law to suppress these plague-laden rats burrowing in the cellars of the social structure. It seems to me that we are more advanced, after all. We know the world and frankly admit it. No book frightens us if it is written by a man whose gifts and whose experience fit him to write for people who demand that good taste alone shall be the line of cleavage between the real and the ideal of life, who knows that we want truth and not polite fibs, but the truths that lie in red roast beef and rich warm wine, not in some nasty mess washed down by rum—nor yet diseased livers and absinthe. From these last, indeed, we have the County Council to protect us, we have only to reject the dull and the imported thin, and to encourage frankly those who add to our knowledge of life and mature our minds. The exceptional man and woman sees, comes into contact with phases of life that the average mortal never brushes. It is, I hold, their duty to tell *all* they know; their only lookout is to tell it for the sane not for the erotic mind. The great writers of the Past all have proved that, given the proper treatment, there is no subject yet evolved on earth that cannot be discussed. But I should say that the great Writers of the Past had never been imported to the United States. Perhaps they were carefully edited and put into drawers first.

By the way, talking of the strange inconsistencies of this country, I have noticed much the same quality in the many American women who have visited England from time to time, some of whom I have known rather well. When they have a lover—and they usually have as far as I am able to judge—they appear to be so frightened that people will find it out. They say and do the most absurd things to throw you off the track. Such unnecessary little explanations and subterfuges—as if any one cared! We are almost frank about our immoralities, carrying things off with a high hand and contemptuously daring anyone to question us. I am not an upholder of immorality, and, so far as I have seen, it carries little happiness with it—neither does virtue, for that matter. What does? Living on a mountain top and dreaming of ideals?—and I would advise women generally to avoid the complications as long as they can, above all the heartache for the man whom no legal tie is always bringing back to them; but I think an insolent admission of it far preferable to hypocrisy, and not nearly so demoralising. All the Americans I have known seemed to me to be constantly striving for something they had not, for a notch above. I believe that originally it was the ideal the young republicans, in common with their republic, strove for, but now I think they are all ashamed of being middle-class and trying to be aristocratic, and they fancy that to be elegantly correct and proper is a part of the game. Oh, dear! Oh, dear! How little they know.

26th

This morning we had a thunder-storm in the midst of a heavy fog—a pure white one like those we call a mist in our country, and bearing no resemblance to the London pea-soup. The lightning flashing through it had an odd and beautiful effect. Later the fog rolled *down* the mountain to the valleys of lower ranges, leaving only a light mist on the mountains and peak opposite. Through this the sun shone gently, and the dense low-looking forests on those distant heights looked as if lightly powdered. I have been down into the forest again. It is wet, but fresher and greener than ever, and full of sweet smells. The balsam when wet, fills the woods with a fragrance that seems to cry aloud of new vitality. Here and there a great tree has fallen, carrying feebler ones with it. To-day I discovered that the ground is covered in many places by a running shrub, that looks like its name, "ground pine." And in other places, on rocks, I found a stiff dark-green moss that looked like a mass of tiny stars. There is so much beauty in these woods one can make only so many discoveries a day. This morning after the storm, I went out by the road instead of the trail, and walked down for a mile or more on those dreadful logs. But that wild magnificent avenue, dropping and turning abruptly, lured me on. Suddenly I saw straight ahead for many miles, and at the end of that lofty perspective was a great mountain, powdered with mist; afterward as I stood watching it, entranced, darkening to a deep rich blue. And between my avenue and that far mountain, was only another lofty valley, high above the level, far from the quick impatient sound of cities. I had not before so fully understood—and revelled in—our isolation.

It sometimes appalls me to be so far from a doctor or a chemist shop, but after all what the Adirondacks cannot do for Bertie no man can, and Agatha has a trunk full of physic. And these *friendly* mountains make disaster and heartbreak seem impossible. That adjective is one of their spirit's keynotes. The post came very late last night and I spent the earlier morning hours reading the newspapers to Bertie. I do not know why Americans should be blamed for their extremes of wealth and poverty, their proneness, indeed, to rush to extremes of all sorts, when they have such an example in their climate. Imagine, Polly, people dying in New York City of the heat, while up here, not three hundred miles away, and in the same State, we were huddled in furs, a roaring fire in every room. During the past nine days we have had the thermometer at 34° and at 86°, we have had sultry thunder-storms on one day and cold rains on the next. To-day it has been heavy and sullen, but yesterday was full of splendour, with an exhilaration in the air that filled Bertie with life and youth once more. His very cheeks seemed to fill out, and his eyes sparkled as they used to do when his legs would not carry him to the cricket-field fast enough.

By the way, dear, Mr. Rogers came up yesterday with several other men. (The families follow in about a week.) They have been fishing since early morn, regardless of the thunder-storm, but have caught little, as the fish in these lakes have much to eat, and grow cleverer every year. Hunter, the lake keeper, told me of their ill-luck, but when I expressed sympathy he shrugged his shoulders.

"They like it," he said; "and them as does 'd set and fish all day in a wash-tub."

But Mr. Rogers arrived quite early yesterday morning, and spent nearly all of the day and

evening with us. Bertie, who improves steadily in spite of all climatic vagaries, was delighted to see him, and they exchanged sporting experiences for several hours.

I have not described Mr. Rogers to you, I think. He is what they call in this country a "great publisher," by which I infer is meant a rich and successful one whose prestige is vastly added to by the fact that he inherited the "great" business, and is not self-made. A young man, an author, who sat at our table on the Oceanic, told me that Mr. Rogers' firm, and three or four others, set the standard for American literature, and that any book with his hall mark on it would be accepted as literature whether the public bought it or not. He has encouraged, helped to create, as it were, the latter-day distinctive American literature, which Bertie and I have so rebelled against these rainy days, and was one of the first to make fashionable the story of locality and dialect. (I think he ought to be hanged for that.) If you don't publish with one of these houses, my informant told me, your struggle will be a long one.

But all that is not very interesting, not nearly so much so as the man himself. He is about fifty-two, I should think, with that tall thin American figure, which when ill-carried is so ungainly and provincial, but very distinguished, if a little stiff, when a man has received the proper training. His face is the coldest I have ever seen; the eyes are grey, the hair and slight moustache nondescript, the features and general outlines finely cut, the whole effect, as I said, cold, and—well, aristocratic. I don't think I ever used the word before I came to this country, but it is always popping off my pen here. It exactly describes Mr. Rogers. He would put a prince of the blood to the blush; refinement (another great American word), fastidiousness, correctness, the just not self-conscious superiority over ordinary mortals, fairly radiate from him in so many cold steady beams. And his voice is admirably modulated. He is a walking protest against American provincialism, from its various accents to that glorious principle that all men are free and equal, which I once read in the Declaration of Independence. (Dad thought so much of that, and used to say it was the highest expression of the Ideal, put into the purest English that ever had been contributed to the literature of Politics.)

Nevertheless, wherever the source of it may lie, Mr. Rogers is charming. Perhaps it is because while he looks as if mortal woman could not fascinate him, he has an air of troubling himself to entertain her. Occasionally he lets her see that her wiles shake his armour just a trifle and that he does not tighten it up again, but permits her glance to penetrate in search of a heart. You don't find a heart—at least I speak for myself—but you find all sorts of pleasant spots, and actually experience a sense of flattery when he laughs heartily at one of your sallies, or keeps his cold eyes fixed steadily on yours as you talk, the reflection of a smile in them. I know that he can be sarcastic and sneering, for I overheard a bout between him and my author acquaintance of the Oceanic; therefore, we who are favoured should find a deep satisfaction in basking in the smiles of this austere and fortunate person. And he certainly can say the most charming things and make you want to please him in return.

As he went through the University of Yale and has alluded to a great-grandfather I should know, even if I had not been told, that he is not a "self-made American"—a variety I am still waiting and wanting to meet. It would be so much like the real thing.

When I thought Bertie had talked enough I took Mr. Rogers for a walk in the forest—and, by the way, it was he who called my attention to the ground pine. He was delightfully solicitous lest I get my feet wet, or catch cold; and when you have been watching over someone else for two years, who is, also, quite the centre of all that sort of thing, you find such solicitude rather fascinating. Mr. Rogers is a widower, by the way, and I have heard that American women train their husbands excellently.

We talked about ferns and trees and birds for a time, and I had the good fortune to see two beautiful birds, one a bright corn-flower blue from tip to tail, the other a deep orange with black wings.

But neither they nor their comrades lifted their voices for a moment. I suppose they have sore throats, poor things. But I did not notice the silence particularly, as we talked all the time. I asked him to tell me something of the people who were coming, and he replied that they were his intimate friends for the most part; that, indeed, forming a club to buy the lake, that they might all be together for six or eight weeks in summer, had been his suggestion. He and a number of other men come for a fortnight in the early spring to fish, and some of the families stay on into September for the deer, but not many, and the lake has rather a bachelor appearance after the last of August.

"I'd like you to define your set," I said, rather bluntly. "I infer you would not condescend to belong to the fashionable frivolous world, and—well —you are not my idea of a Bohemian, nor yet exactly middle-class—I mean what I imagine the American middle class to be."

"No," he said, smiling, "we are not fashionable in the '400' meaning of the word, nor are we Bohemians, nor yet middle class. The set to which I belong, if you must have all the facts—and you have only to command me for all the facts on any subject that I understand—embraces what might vulgarly be called the successful brains of New York—and those of other cities which have come to us to stay. Mind you, I mean successful in the right way: editors, publishers and authors, who aim only to give the world the most fastidious expression of the American spirit, a few artists—although, as a rule, they herd together; but there are several fine illustrators who class themselves with us; also people who do not pretend to give to the public, but who love literature, music, and art of all sorts and prefer meeting people of brains and refinement to associating with a class which thinks of nothing but spending money."

"In short," I exclaimed, "you are the true aristocracy of New York."

"Yes," he replied unsuspiciously. "I think we are. There was a time when to be in the fashionable set of New York argued birth and breeding; money was no passport in those days. But to-day there is no other; the '400,' as it is absurdly called, has so few family trees that they could all be stored in one linen closet; it is money, money—and—consequently—the sort of vulgarity one most wants to avoid."

"But many of your set must have money," I said, determined to get to the bottom of these puzzling distinctions; "all of these cottages must have cost a great deal of money, particularly on top of a mountain with corduroy roads; and the keeper has often let fall remarks from which I have inferred that no economy is practised by your friends."

"Oh, yes," he replied with that flicker of humour in his eyes and voice which makes him transiently human, "there are several respectable millions among us, but the point is, we none of us are disgustingly rich. We are not known by our wealth, it is not invariably mentioned coincidently with our names, and, indeed, we stand on quite another basis. And many of these delightful people you will meet in a few days are only comfortably off—although they all have enough to entertain with in their own individual fashion."

"You don't mean that some are eccentric?" I demanded. "Surely you would not countenance eccentricity."

"Certainly not!" he exclaimed, quite as emphatically as I had expected; "no cultivated person ever was eccentric and 'Bohemians' are welcome to the monopoly of it for their vulgar advertising. I mean that each entertains according to his —or shall I say her?—means, and manages so to stamp her affairs with her own individuality that one never thinks of the amount expended."

"It sounds very alluring, but a little alarming," I said. "Do they *all* come up here?"

"Oh, no, and many more men than women. Our women have their delicious frivolities, I assure you, and are always running over to Europe to replenish their really splendid wardrobes, while others seem never to tire of travel. But those who do come are very representative and I want you to like them better than those whose highest ambition is to get into your own set in England."

"I have met some charming Americans," I replied, "and they always seemed bright and full of talk. It was only when they tried to be English that I didn't like them. Bertie adores American women, but whether he will like this superior intellectual variety——"

"Oh, do not form an erroneous impression," he said, hastily. "I assure you they do not in any way resemble the poor Bostonians who have been so severely caricatured. They have accomplished the happy combination of intellectual activity and appreciation, with a light worldliness and a love of the best that their money and opportunities can buy, which makes them unique in their country."

"I infer that your set is quite exclusive, difficult to get into."

"It is—much more so than the fashionable set, for money is far more plentiful in this country than that peculiar combination of brains, culture, and pecuniary success which I may say is the hall-mark of our set. I have a theory that the right sort of gifts always is successful; by that I mean those gifts which are distinctively American in the highest sense—Americanism in all its wonderful distinctiveness, but polished, refined, cultivated, purified of dross. The exponents of it naturally are successful with the large increasing number throughout the country who possess the instinct to rise higher and strive for the best; therefore, when these exponents are gathered together anywhere, they form a fastidious circle which excludes inharmonious spirits, and constitutes what is now the real aristocracy of the country. But, I can assure you, we are perfectly normal," he added, with his rare delightful smile. "We dine and wine each other, have many a game of poker, love sport, have our boxes at the opera, and know the world pretty thoroughly."

"It sounds profoundly interesting," I said, but when I repeated the conversation to Bertie he growled that it was "jolly rot."

"I shall like the men if they are like Rogers," he added; "for he's a jolly good sort inside that chain-mail armour of his; but I feel sure I shall hate the women. I'll be bound they are rotters, every one of them—the personification of their self-conscious provincial literature. If they are I'll make a public scandal by flirting with Jemima."

27th

Curiously enough I ended my last entry with Jemima's name, and I have just had another characteristic conversation with her. Last night I awakened suddenly out of a sound sleep, my mind alert with the idea that something had happened to Bertie. I sprang out of bed and opened the door. At once I heard Parker moving about Bertie's room—his own adjoins it and he is devotion itself, the good soul. I was not one minute, I can assure you, getting into a wrapper and crossing the hall. Parker opened the door for me, and when I saw his anxious face I pushed him aside and hastened to the bed. There lay Bertie white and gasping; and Polly, when I saw that towel I thought for a moment I should faint. He has not had a hemorrhage now for so long that I had fallen indolently into the belief he never would have another. I had put those dreadful towels—which for two years were spread all over my imagination—quite out of my mind. What brought on this attack I cannot imagine—but I am not going to horrify you with details. I put my arm under his head and sat there all night. He was not able to get up until this afternoon and I did not leave his room. When, however, he was in his hammock on the veranda, with Agatha reading the *Times* to him, I slipped away to the woods, for I wanted to be alone.

I was too tired to walk far, but when I felt quite alone I sat down on a rock in those friendly depths and cried bitterly. The future, after this really radiant interval, seemed doubly dark and uncertain. How again could I ever be *sure* that Bertie would get well? The doctor said that the Adirondacks were the last hope, and if Bertie wears them out——

Suddenly I became conscious that some one was staring at me. I rose hastily, dabbing my eyes, and confronted Jemima. Her mouth and eyes were wide open.

"You ain't cryin'?" she gasped. "You! Land o' livin'!" and then she recovered herself and added apologetically, "I guess you didn't hear me comin', these wood trails is so soft. Won't you set down again? I wouldn't go back with my eyes red if I was you, because there are two or three gentlemen to your camp and they think you're so beautiful I'd hate to have them see you when you ain't."

I meekly resumed my seat and Jemima perched herself on a log opposite. I was rather glad of the diversion, now that my grief had spent itself, and Jemima always amuses me.

"You have not gone home?" I asked.

"No, ma'am. I'm not goin'. I'm goin' to stay and help Mis' Hunter. There's an awful lot of work here in summer, and her other hired girl's not very strong."

"Well, I am glad you have found a place to suit you. I presume you eat with Mrs. Hunter and her family?"

"Yes'm." Then she added, with uncontrollable curiosity, "What were you cryin' for, anyway?"

"My brother was very ill again last night and I am terribly anxious about him."

"And do you high-toned English folks with

titles love each other and have troubles just like us plain folks?" she demanded.

I could not help laughing. "Why not?" I asked.

"Oh, 'cause you seem just like people in books, not like real live folks. Seems as if you oughter just sail round with peeple waitin' on you and never have any everyday thoughts and feelin's."

"I assure you we are very human," I said drily, "and perhaps we feel both joy and sorrow more keenly than you do. There is every reason why we should."

"But I'll bet you never called your parents mommer and popper."

Of course I laughed again. "No, because those musical endearments do not happen to be customary in my country. I do not remember calling my mother anything, for she died when I was two years old. But we both called my father Dad."

She gasped, "Naw, you didn't. You never called a dook Dad."

"Oh, but we did," I exclaimed, glowing as certain memories rose; "and when he used to come home from long tiring sessions in the Upper House, or Cabinet meetings—he was a very conscientious legislator, and had held more than one position of great responsibility—he loved to lie down on the floor, and let us run all over him. It was my brother's delight to polish Dad's boots with his toothbrush, and I used to barber him with my doll's scissors. When we got too big for all that he gave us even more of his time, every hour he could spare; he even helped tutor us, and he never went to the continent without us. While we were studying he never went at all, and during our holidays—which were usually his own—he either took us travelling or lived in the country with us. He adored us and we adored him."

"My! Well, I don't know as I ever seen any farmer make such a fuss over his kids as that, but farmers are terrible busy."

"So was my father, but he knew the exact value of everything in life, and that is the reason he made so much of love."

This was beyond her, and she merely remarked: "I suppose you took on terrible when he died."

"I didn't 'take on,' but no words ever can express my misery."

"And do you have other kinds of trouble too? Do your fellers ever go back on you? I don't mean *you*; I guess you ain't in any danger of havin' your heart broke; but I mean other grand ladies with titles? Do they ever get left like us common folks."

"I have known a good many to 'get left,'" I replied, smiling at certain reminiscences, "Human nature is pretty much the same in all spheres—more so, perhaps in ours, where people have so much flung at their feet that fickleness is a natural consequence."

"I guess men is fickle everywhere. I know several that has gone back on real nice girls just because they seen another girl they liked better. I'd *hate* to get left! My!"

"You speak for your sex," I said. "I have known many who looked indifferent, but I never knew one who was."

"I guess I'd try to look as if I didn't care, but I guess the louder I laughed the more people'd suspicion I was all water inside. You look real nice now. Your nose ain't red any more; but your eyes 's got rings under them. I don't see why you need to set up nights when the Dook's got that there gentleman, Mr. Parker, to wait on him."

"Well, I am his sister," you know, I said lightly, and then, as I was tired, rather, of Jemima, I went back to the house. Bertie seems much better to-night, and is now asleep. I have hung branches of balsam all over his room. They look so brilliantly green against the light-brown varnished wood which defines every spike. And their fragrance! It ought to fill Bertie's poor lungs with new life. I am going for a row with Mr. Rogers to-morrow morning, and if he says anything characteristic I'll write it out for your benefit. He has promised already to spend our first autumn in Yorkshire with us, so you will be the more interested when you meet him.

28th.

Our conversation was political and I must relate it to you. But first the morning row. It was so beautiful. It was like drifting through crystal. My distant peak was a monstrous turquois. The thick woods about us showed every shade of green. The honeysuckle is gone, but the moss is richer than ever, and now and again one glimpses a purple lily. In little bays there are water-lilies, and on the miniature islands a wildness, a tangle of fern and young trees, that is indescribable. In some places there is a good deal of pollen on the water, but the greater part of the lake's surface is golden-brown and bright. The only blot on the lovely picture is the too frequent dead spruce. A blight attacked them a year or two ago, and they still look like church spires, but crumbling and gray.

We did not talk politics on the lake—Heaven forbid!—we drifted from nature to art, of which he has a delightful knowledge; but I won't repeat all that as he did not say anything particularly illuminating. It was at luncheon that the subject of politics came up; I forget exactly how, although as I discuss our own with Bertie and Agatha daily, and have lived in a political atmosphere all my life, I suppose they never are far from the surface of my mind. Daddy always took a certain interest in American politics, so I knew something of them before I came, and heaven knows their newspapers would not leave one long in ignorance.

Oh, I remember how the conversation began. After expatiating upon the beauty of the lake and the silence of these mountain tops—positively when we stopped talking there had not been a sound but the gurgle of water against the boat—I repeated what I remember writing to you about the climate of this country setting a bad example to the people in the matter of extremes. Mr. Rogers smiled quickly, and looked at me with his steady, and—shall I write it?—*approving*—gaze.

"There is some food for reflection in that," he said. "But—how much do you know of this country?" he added gently—I mean his voice took all sting out of the words.

I told him what I have just written. I added

that I was anxious to learn more, and that I had been saturating myself in its press and literature. Here Bertie grunted, and I said something hastily about the delicious speckled trout Mr. Rogers had sent us which we were then eating.

"And you found the same extremes there," said Mr. Rogers, quite ignoring my diversion, which I am positive he understood. "Nevertheless, we have a very large middle class, and there are certain sections of the country where the climate is very temperate—California, for instance."

"I thought that State had perpetual snow in the north and perpetual summer in the south, and eight months of dry weather and four months of rain. A cousin of mine has ranched there for ten years. Surely that bears out the national predilection for violent or sharply drawn contrasts."

"Well, you rather have me there," he admitted gracefully. "One gets so in the habit of saying certain things about a country just as one goes on commenting upon a man's cleverness after one ought to appreciate the fact that a little frank analysis would prick the bubble. Florida is perpetual summer with an occasional blizzard; but even that bears out your theory."

"As to your middle-class," I asked, "don't they all intend to be upper-class some day? Are any of them contented to be middle-class, generation in and generation out?"

"I don't know much about them," he said carelessly, "but the American instinct certainly is to progress. You might indeed call progress our watch-word. That is the reason this Bryan hue and cry won't wash. His democracy is merely a fancy word for plebeianism. The sixteen to one nonsense has not received any more attention from that faction of the press that booms Bryan than his everlasting farmer poor man pose, and his plain homely wife, who sweeps off the veranda as the newspaper correspondents approach the unpretentious mansion. Do they suppose for a moment that any typical American wants an unbarbered shirt-sleeved episode in the White House, with a follower of Dolly Madison, Miss Harriet Lane, or their own popular and irreproachable Mrs. Cleveland, bustling about at six in the morning dusting the White House furniture or making gingerbread in the kitchen? Not for a moment. It would mean retrogression, and they know it. They have no desire to be the laughing-stock of other countries, to have the President of the United States ill at ease and vulgar in the presence of Ambassadors. Just as every American is animated by the desire to better himself, to get ahead of his neighbours, so is he equally ambitious for his country. I should be willing to wager my last dollar that if Bryan did reach the White House, with his malodorous tribe elbowing all decent people out of it, every self-respecting man who had voted for him would read the press reports with a snort of disgust. Backsliding will never work, for we have not reached the summit of our civilisation yet."

"I don't think much of the man you've got in now," said Bertie. "He takes an imposing photograph, but I infer that he is a sort of human mask for Mr. Hanna."

"McKinley is, as yet, the great historical puzzle without a key," said Mr. Rogers, evasively;

"but we do want, now and always, a gentleman in the White House, and with the many men in the country of birth and breeding, education and distinguished ability, it argues a terrible disease in our body politic that we cannot put the right man in the right place and keep him there."

"Have you ever made the effort?" I asked pointedly, for I had heard things. "You, and all those who think as you do?"

As I had expected, he shook his head. "No. I cannot face the filth of American politics. I touched them once during a great reform spurt in New York, several years ago, and I feel as if my hands are not clean yet. I shall not offend your ears by a description of the people by whom we were jostled at the polls, nor what we had to handle in attempting to push any reform measure through."

"Good gad!" exclaimed Bertie, "where would England be if we had funked the business of reform fifty years ago? My father took off his coat and waded into the filth—which was a long sight worse than yours—up to his neck. He and others like him made the country what it is to-day. Upon my word, Rogers, you make me sick."

Mr. Rogers, who is used to Bertie's plain speech, smiled and replied politely.

"Would that we had a great force like your father, to push us into the right path. But I am afraid the great majority of would-be reformers feel as I do."

"It's your roast beef," growled Bertie, scowling at his. "It's only about half the weight of ours and only gives a chap half the blood he needs."

"It is more delicate and easier to digest than yours."

"For American stomachs—that's the point."

"Are there no gentlemen in politics?" I asked, hurriedly, for Bertie can be rude in a way that Americans cannot understand.

"Unquestionably. There are quite a few in the Senate, but in them the political passion is stronger than their fastidiousness. Even the honours and the fame they may win cannot compensate for the dirt they are obliged to come into contact with every week in the year."

"Well, all I can say is, that you haven't the true sporting instinct in this country," said Bertie. "Men of the same sort ought to stand by each other. If a certain number of gentlemen are willing to hold their noses and plunge in for the good of the country it's your duty to close up the ranks behind them and keep the stink as far in the background as possible."

Poor Mr. Rogers blushed and looked most distressed, for that word is tabooed in this country, dear, and I doubt if the poor man ever heard it before. He saw my eyes dance, and gave me a look of such pained surprise that it was my turn to be distressed, for it is so cruel to shatter a man's ideals! Bertie pursued all unconsciously:

"Can't you see it from my point of view, Rogers? Ain't you in the habit of standing by your friends in this country?"

"Certainly, Duke," replied Mr. Rogers, suavely; he had quite recovered himself. "I think you will find Americans as loyal as any men on earth."

"Not unless they go the whole length and stand by their own class when there is such a crying need for help as there is here. I suppose there's a respectable number of gentlemen in the country, ain't there?"

"A very large number. A highly respectable proportion of the seventy millions. I am constrained to make that admission, even though I hand you another weapon."

"It is a weapon, by gad. And I'd like jolly well to understand your supineness. Perhaps you'll wake up all in a moment and fling off your coats and go to work."

"I wish I could think so. What we lack most, I fancy, is a leader, for unquestionably we have caste loyalty. But when all is said the upper class in this country is small—compared to the vast sub-stratum—and the country is so huge that homogeneity is almost impossible. So far, every man has made his fight alone; and there *is* something pathetic in it—come to think of it."

"I think those who have made the fight must be ripping fine men, and I'd like to meet some of them. Will any of them come up here this summer?"

Mr. Rogers shook his head. "I am sorry, but we do not happen to have any politicians in the club. I thought it over carefully and concluded that it was better not, for they cannot avoid knowing objectionable people who might manage to get themselves invited here, too."

Again, I interposed before Bertie could answer. "What becomes of your law of progress? If it is as inborn and inevitable—unhinderable—as you say, why does it not sweep your class in its current? Surely that class is increased from year to year by ambitious recruits whose offspring will be as cultivated as you are to-day—that is part of your law of progress. It seems to me that a natural instinct should force you and your sort to labour to keep yourselves high above the masses and fill the great public offices of the country."

As he turned to me the light in his eyes was almost warm and I felt as if I had said something really clever. That is his little way.

"That was very well reasoned," he said, "and your theory has certain facts to substantiate it, inasmuch as public life does receive recruits from the upper-class from year to year. Perhaps, some day, under the stress of a great menace, the entire class will throw in its weight. But just now—merely to give the country a stiffer man than McKinley—I am afraid they will not. We are such optimists, our luck has had such few facers, and just now we are so prosperous. It is only a dream to imagine the best in both parties suddenly deserting and uniting; for the best men seem to avoid leadership and notoriety; it is only by doing so that they can find a comparatively clean path through the political muck."

Bertie shrugged his shoulders and pushed back his chair. "You look well in that tweed outfit and those leggings, Rogers," he said, "but you'd look a jolly sight better in your shirt sleeves and with mud on your boots. You and the rest of your dilettante class are living in a Fool's Paradise, and when you're choking over your first nasty mess of Bryanism you'll wish you'd taken off your coat while you had a valet to assist you. For my part I'm rather keen on Bryan getting in. I want to see a real democracy. What you've got now is neither one thing nor the other. Say what you like you have an enormously large aristocratic class, a class which is always looking round for somebody to snub and which holds itself immeasurably above the masses. You'll be a monarchy yet with every title that ever was heard of, and American inventions to boot. The result of your Trust system will be two classes—the wealthy and the helpless poor. The hour the wealthy class feels that it is strong enough it will make for a court and a nobility. And a nice mess you'll make of it."

"Well," said Mr. Rogers, laughing, "it will be infinitely preferable to Populism, and it certainly will be all in the law of progress. Every American, even the Populist, wants to be rich, and as soon as he is rich he wants to be cultivated beyond his original condition. After that stage democracy is a retrogression and there is nothing to do but go on and become an aristocrat. As you say, when there are enough of them, monarchy is only a step further."

And there the conversation ended.

I think this letter is thick enough to go—don't you?

Ever yours,

HELEN.

P. S. The evening post came just after I had finished, and brought me a welcome letter from you. I open this for a few lines of answer. Freddy must be *mad.* I hope to God, V. R. will keep his head. Can't you persuade him to go to South Africa? As long as you have made up your mind not to see him till all is over, I should think it would be a positive relief to have him where you *can't* see him. And if there is danger—do pack him off. Who do you suppose can be putting Freddy up to such devilment?—that creature? She may see revenge in it. Do be careful. If you came a cropper now—I read your letter to Bertie and he says he wishes you would chuck the whole thing and come over here to us, and wait patiently for Freddy's several diseases to finish him. But I told him he never had been deeply in love—and he said he was jolly glad he hadn't. Well, I'll say a prayer for you, out in the forest—although I don't believe it does a bit of good to pray for anyone but yourself. My theory is that by the intense absorption, concentration, and faith of prayer, you put yourself into magnetic communication with the great Divine Force pervading the Universe and draw some of its strength into yourself. Sometimes the strength is physical, or rather is directed to physical ends, as when one prays a pain out; and at others one draws strength enough to endure and overcome anything—but not without that intense concentration. The mere babbling of a petition does no good. There you have the result of my inner observations. Try it for yourself.

Letter IV

From the Lady HELEN POLE *to the Countess of* EDGE *and* ROSS.

Boulder Lake,
July 2d

THE people have been here several days now, and the lake looks very gay. When the men are not fishing the boats are filled with the children, ducky little things in white pinnys and bright ribbons. I am going to have them all over by themselves for luncheon some day, for, so far, I like them better than their "mommers." The men are a well turned-out lot, but look tired, and—anæmic. So far, I have seen little of them, as Mr. Rogers has delayed bringing them over to call—possibly until the mountain air has made them feel a little more fit. New York is said to be unbearably hot, and, you know, the rich men in this country work as hard as the poor ones. Did I tell you that they all dine at the Club House? This cottage would have been impracticable for us did not Mr. Rogers have an invalid mother who could not leave the house—which is quite apart from the others—for days at a time. Therefore, we have here a complete kitchen, pantry, etc., and are quite independent of what would be to us all a detestable arrangement, even if Bertie were well. He is quite fit again, by the way, and has several times been fishing with Mr. Rogers. He has met a number of the men and says he likes most of them, but has taken a violent dislike to an author that this admiring circle has made a fool of, and longs to be well enough to kick him. He likes the women as little as I do.

They have all called on us. They came singly and in battalions. I have a general impression of thin carefully modulated voices, fluffy well-groomed hair, delicate features, light eyes, a discontented expression—which is reflected in their voices—an unbounded self-confidence, an annoying and persistent self-consciousness, and the most perfect gowns imaginable. In the morning they wear the triggest serge or tweed costumes, on hot days linen of various colours, in the afternoon they flit about in pretty lawns, and in the evening they are very smart indeed—several of them called after dinner.

As they will doubtless flit in and out of my

letters very often I will do my poor best to introduce several of them to you that you may see some sort of object behind the names.

The four that have impressed me most so far are Mrs. Chenoweth, the wife of a "great" editor; Mrs. Hammond, the wife of a "great" art publisher; Mrs. Laurence, a "wonderfully successful" authoress, and Miss Simpson, the editor of a "great" woman's magazine; her name is Margaret E. Simpson. She left a card!

Mrs. Chenoweth is the least objectionable of the four, because in spite of her sleepy self-content and air of gentle superiority, there is something sweet and domestic about her, and occasionally her eyes seem to fill up with sympathy; and there is a placid note in her voice, unique in her "set." She talked about her husband most of the time, and left me wondering how the universe had room for two magazines. But if she did not show so plainly that she was used to flattery and adulation I'd like her rather.

Mrs. Hammond sits forward on the edge of the chair and talks all the time. Her small expensively dressed figure looks as if her eager soul might burst through it at any moment, every nerve seems to be on the jump at once; and as for her face I followed its play of expression bewildered. She is what is vulgarly and aptly called a "gusher." She gushed steadily for three quarters of an hour about literature and art. Art is her passion; she almost faints before a great painting, and etching gives her thrills which she can express in French only, so inadequate is our commonplace language. She told me with great pride that foreigners always took her for a French woman, so perfect was her mastery of the language; and when I told her it was a relief to meet an American who was not proud of being one, she looked embarrassed and said of course she wouldn't really be anything else. She then leaped into the midst of literature, but somewhat to my surprise had little to say about American. I was given to understand how deeply read the ambitious active little lady was in English, French, Russian, German, Norwegian, Danish, Italian, and even Spanish classics, old and new, but her only reference to those of her own country was at the end of the homily, when she gushed out eulogies of Mrs. Laurence, and Mr. Henry Walker Rolfs.

"Mrs. Laurence is quite the most brilliant woman in America," she assured me. "Of course you know her novels — they sell immensely — so full of style and brilliant pictures and illusiveness and delicate satire and purity of thought; but she is even more fascinating herself. I don't believe there is a woman living who can say so many clever things in the course of an hour, and she is quite a beauty, and dresses deliciously—superlatively—even for New York. And Mr. Rolfs! Of course you love his work—he has the immense sales he deserves to have — such style, such word-painting, such spiritual insight —real interpretation of God. He is so great I involuntarily lower my voice to speak to him, and I think the two most wonderful sights I ever have witnessed are Henry Walker Rolfs *fishing* and *eating*. It seems incredible that he *can* do anything just like other men. But indeed he spends most of his time in the woods alone—thinking,

thinking, interpreting Nature and God. Oh, I know, dear Lady Helen, you will be perfectly delighted with all our friends, and find us *very* different from those exaggerated Americans who are constantly bombarding London Society with their vulgar millions."

"You *are* different," I thought. "I never dreamed of anything in Heaven or on Earth like you."

Now, as it happens, Mrs. Laurence's and Mr. Rolfs' books are Bertie's and my pet abominations. We think the former trivial, thin, and insincere to a degree that her pretty manner in no way compensates for, and Mr. Rolfs equally insincere and anæmic, and laboured and dull in the bargain. His style certainly is polished to an unusual degree, even for an American, and he *engraves*—never paints—quite wonderful pictures. But his characters never come to life for a moment and there is no atmosphere or perspective in his work—it is flat against the canvas—like the paintings of the Chinese. Read —— —— ——* and —— ——*

* Deletions by the publisher.

and see if you do not agree with me. By the way, he is the man Bertie wants to kick.

I will describe Miss Simpson next, for as Mrs. Laurence is always the last to arrive or to call on a new-comer, I will reserve for her the *éclat* she covets. Miss Simpson is extremely handsome, tall, massive, with brown strong-looking hair, grey eyes with an expression of haughty surprise—as if lesser mortals were in the habit of taking liberties with her—a goodish complexion, a rather thick round profile, and a small hard mouth with a downward bend. Success is emblazoned upon her, as well as gratified power and ambition. She began life, I am informed by one of her enthusiastic admirers, as a clerk in a bank "out West," but soon —feeling that her education and gifts fitted her for the higher life—"came East" and engaged in journalism. I cannot express the pride with which —Mrs. Chenoweth, I think it was—told me that Miss Simpson had never brushed her skirts against yellow journalism; although she came here quite unknown and from that hybrid region known as the "West," it appears that her instincts were aristocratic from the first. She made herself invaluable on one of the "very best papers," gradually wedged her way—I fear that expression is my own—into conservative circles, dropping such acquaintances as were detrimental, and finally graduated as a full-fledged editor of a woman's magazine, capitalised by an eccentric but appreciative millionairess. It was only a year or so ago, however, that she "arrived" in this upper and rarified stratum, and is here not as a member, but as the guest of Mrs. Chenoweth. It must be a jolly sensation to have striven for something so high above your reach and finally achieved it. What contempt for those left below, what constant self-gratulation. Miss Simpson quite chilled me with the silent hauteur of her manner, the level dissecting rays of her fine eyes. She holds herself aloft, as it were, with the rigid spine of the traditional queen; but let me confide to you, Polly dear, she looks like a successful business woman, *tout même*, not at all like what I fancy she wishes to resemble. And if she is a success as a business person I will venture to say she is a failure as a woman. Her ambition has been so positive, so undeviating, so remorseless (I have listened to six biographies of her), that the human attributes have withered up just as unused muscles do. I asked Bertie what he thought of her, and he said he had more respect for a harlot, as women had been created for two offices only—mothers and strumpets. "If a woman fills neither of these offices she is a failure and had better be dead." That is a nice primitive view and I'd enjoy hearing it exploded in the midst of this select camp. They exult in Miss Simpson's virtue —it is monumental—and has flourished like a green bay tree in spite of New York and its mysterious temptations. Personally, I should say her virtue was purely a negative quality due to absence of temptation, within and without. So far, she is rather in this well-uniformed set than of it; she speaks with a slight twang and expresses herself in rather shoppy language. But she is ambitious and determined, and no doubt will adapt herself in time.

Mrs. Laurence! She was of those who called after dinner. She was in full evening dress—black

—and came into the room with a rustling of skirts I never have known equalled. I should say that her train had at least six inner silk flounces and it switched about on the bare floor like an angry tiger's tail. I think she changed her seat seven times and always with that portentous rustling. I noticed that this occurred whenever someone else had spoken consecutively for five minutes. She is a pretty woman, and the old word "elegant" exactly expresses her; our grandmothers would have called her "most genteel." She has a cloud of cendré hair, softly curled, and the pretty contrast of baby blue eyes, although they, as well as her red thin lips, are petulant in expression. Her features are delicate to the vanishing point and her figure very graceful. She is, undoubtedly, an old hand at aristocracy, for her voice, in spite of its fretful note, is exquisitely trained, her language polished in the extreme, with every comma and semicolon in its proper place; and her manner quite that of the grande dame of the American novel. She mentioned eighteen people of title she had met in England—among them Milly Seton—

and alluded, with a fretful sigh, to her many visits in England's "enchanting homes."

"I wish I could marry an Englishman," she said, with her little pout, "I have had so many offers from my own countrymen but not one from an Englishman—I think it is too bad! Of course I shall marry again, I'm so feminine and I hate work—I always am so amused when the critics rave over my quick brilliant style and verbal felicities; I grind out every sentence and hate the very sight of the paper. I want to marry a rich man who will pet me and leave me nothing to do but to be charming and to dress exquisitely. That is all a woman ever was made for, not to write tiresome books that other people think clever. Of course, I am glad I am such a success; but I'm sure I'd a great deal rather be you. You look the real thing, and we are all just creditable imitations. I am sure I was English once—in a former state—I feel so *at home* when I am in one of your old castles, surrounded by people who are all that I should like to be, and I am such a success with them; I could not be more so if I were to the manor born; I am sure I cannot understand why some flower of nobility has not fairly flung himself and his hereditary acres at my feet."

All this before Bertie, and it reads like the most engaging candour; but as she fairly breathes insincerity and self-consciousness one does not believe *anything* she says, and I think she knows it. When she left, I asked Bertie if she was feminine enough to suit him, and he said that she was a cat, whose proper place was in a fancy basket in the drawing-room; no English Tom, at least, would ever invite her on to the roof. Bertie is coarse at times, but nobody can deny that he is expressive.

Polly, are these people merely snobs? What do you make of them? You write me, you dear thing, that my letters are profoundly interesting to you and that I pop the people I meet right into your imagination. I am so glad, for they certainly interest me. It is like living in a novel—an American one, it is true, but fresh and new, and full of unsolved problems to the mere outsider. They certainly are not snobs in the old meaning of the word, not in the least like those of their country who work so hard to be taken up by us, and imitate our manners and pronunciation. No, they are either snobs and something more, or not snobs at all, but a different manifestation of the struggle for the Ideal. That sounds better, at all events; let them go at that.

Mr. Rogers told me that they all admired me very much, but found me rather "cold and haughty." I could not help laughing aloud, and of course Mr. Rogers understands. You know how shy and frightened of strangers I am, a failing I never shall get over. I suppose that makes me sit cold and rigid when, in reality, I would give a good deal to talk as fast as they do—and as I can when I know and like people well enough. I did feel myself growing stiffer and stiffer as Mrs. Hammond gushed, but that was quite natural, it seems to me. Agatha was rather bewildered at first by their facile and unrestrained speech, but she likes them all, dear soul. She takes them on their face value, and they each gave her material to admire without looking for it.

July 4th.

Yesterday I went to the Club House to dinner; Mr. Rogers rowed me over and back. The dining-room is rather pretty, with three long tables. Mr. Rogers sits at the head of the middle table and I sat on his right. Mrs. Laurence was very "brilliant." Every time she began to speak, and that was usually, everybody stopped talking and leaned forward. "I would not miss a word," whispered my neighbour. "Her wit *lives* on the tip of her tongue and never sleeps." I cannot transcribe her brilliancy, Polly dear, because it is of the quality known as elusive, not the old-fashioned kind that you repeat and hand down to your grand-children. She delivered her witticisms, too, at the rate of one every three minutes, and I should like to know *who* could keep track of them. I wondered if her fascinating, fretful, spoilt-darling voice has not something to do with the belief that she is witty and unique. For, Polly, I must admit it, she bored me to death, and at times I felt like protesting. But I scarcely opened my mouth; and I don't doubt they think I am stupid and have a typical English lack of the sense of humour. But I do not blame Mrs. Laurence, and do not dislike her as much as I did, for she is merely a hothouse product, forced into an abnormal artificial growth by these foolish people, who must have their lion, or the times would be out of joint.

The great Mr. Rolfs sat opposite me, but he does not go in for brilliancy; to amuse, he doubtless holds, is beneath the dignity of a great mind. He ate his excellent dinner in a ponderous and solemn manner, oblivious of the admiring eyes riveted upon him when Mrs. Laurence was not speaking; his vision introspective, as if he still pondered the last of the Almighty's confidences, and, when spoken to, responding with a sweet but absent graciousness. I wanted to throw my ice-cream at him—only it was very good ice-cream, made of crushed strawberries, and would have been wasted on such a muff.

In the fine large cosey living-room afterward they *played intellectual games*. My dear, I thought I should die. I could not leave in common decency before ten o'clock, and for a mortal hour I listened to the brilliant Mrs. Laurence exhibit the most wonderful fertility, ingenuity, and resource, switching her noisy tail round the polished floor till it hissed like a harassed snake. She was in white embroidered mousseline de soie and silk—Oh, much and noisy silk—and she wore turquoises, and altogether looked like an advertisement for the calling of letters. Her rival, Mr. Rolfs, had retreated from the field—probably to the roof—and I don't exaggerate when I say that the others never took their eyes off her, with the exception of some of the men, who went to sleep. Finally, I could stand it no longer, and I went over and sat down by Miss Simpson, who seemed to be as much out of it as I was, and who, since she had failed to catch the spirit of the thing, was endeavouring to look superior to contemptible frivolities.

"A very brilliant woman," I said, beginning with the obvious.

"I guess there's not much use disputing that fact," she answered with an expression which conveyed to me that this remark was intended as grim humour. "And if she were not, she's clever enough to make people think so."

"Do you admire that particular form of brilliancy?" I asked, longing to hear her say what I thought; but she answered emphatically:

"I admire success. When you strive for that and get it you're entitled to all the applause there is, whether it is the brand some one else would strike out for or not. I have succeeded in my way and she acknowledges it and me; therefore, I take off my hat to her. I have aimed for something more solid; but because I prefer to spend my money on oil paintings there is no law against my patting the dainty water-colourist on the back. And I do—every time. So long as a person does not get in my way he can have a whole road to himself and welcome."

Here was genuine frankness, no doubt of that. She prided herself upon it and was quite aware that she was impressing me, but it was the sort of insolent frankness that compels belief. I asked her if she was not the author of——* which I had

* Elimination by the publisher.

read recently, and she thawed perceptibly and even gave me a very charming smile. To draw her on I praised the novel highly—it was clever but sketchy and betrayed no knowledge of the world whatever—and she thanked me very pleasantly and admitted that she hoped to make an even greater success with her second one.

"I have had some very fortunate experiences since I wrote that," she said. "I have watched a love affair progress right under my nose, and I was visiting a friend of mine when her husband was accidentally killed. She was a wonderful psychological study in her grief!" and she set her mouth, as if overcome by the responsibility of her own brain.

"Good God!" I exclaimed.

She turned slowly and gave me a look of such haughty inquiry that I almost wilted.

"I beg your pardon," I said meekly, "but it seemed to me rather a shocking advantage to take. Really—how *could* you?"

"Of course, as you don't write you don't know that a true artist sees copy in everything, that human nature was made to be studied, and that when a palpitating leaf is torn out and flung into an author's lap he would be seven different kinds of fool if he didn't read it."

"I can understand now why your literature is heartless," I retorted, "for you kill your own heart before you write it. But, if you go in for brain-picking to that extent, why do you so persistently ignore the motive power of human life—sex?"

"Oh," she said with an accent of contempt and disgust. "*We* don't want any of that. We leave that to the decadent civilisations. It's not the fashion in this country. *We're* healthy."

"I think you are decidedly unhealthy," I made bold to retort—"and if you don't take care the water in your blood will prevent you from attaining full growth. Well, at all events you will escape decadency," I added lightly. "Good night."

I crossed the room toward Mr. Rogers, determined upon retreat, but was intercepted by Mrs. Chenoweth. She gave me so sweet a smile that I was obliged to pause.

"Do sit and talk to me a moment," she said.

"I have been longing to see more of you. I am glad you were so kind to Miss Simpson. I think she is a type that should be encouraged and I am doing all I can for her. Of course she is what is called self-made, she has no family-tree, but, as Junot said, 'Some of us must be ancestors'—you remember that is quoted in the Rémusat Memoirs; delightful reading, whether they are authentic or not. I thought I would tell you just how Miss Simpson stands, lest you should wonder a little at her accent and stiffness; but she is so estimable and capable and altogether superior—and bound to go so far—I am sure you will think I am right to take her up."

"I don't see any reason in the world why you shouldn't," I replied, "and it certainly has interested me very much to meet her. I really must go, if you don't mind. I am so very tired."

On the way back I told Mr. Rogers of my conversation with Miss Simpson and of my disgust. He smiled good naturedly.

"Oh, that is only the zeal of the amateur," he said. "They get less shoppy every year."

"But don't they lose a good deal meanwhile?" I asked.

"Well, perhaps," he admitted.

The children are making such a racket with firecrackers I can scarcely think, but I send you much love and sympathy. HELEN

Letter V

From the Lady HELEN POLE *to the Countess of* EDGE *and* ROSS.

Boulder Lake,
July 10th

DO not imagine, Polly, that I have given up my solitary ramblings in the forest. I enjoy them more than ever; and their *soundlessness* after the eternal babble which pervades the lake—I am afraid I am not grateful for all the kind attentions I receive—is simply delicious. Leaves, green leaves everywhere, rioting to my knees and hanging in the air. You never notice the slender branches, only the delicate fairy curtain they hang between the dark stems of the trees. And the ferns, and the ground pine, and the green stars of that moss that covers ground and rock, and the rich velvet moss, shading from a dark green to one that is almost white, that covers the fallen trees, and the incomparable solitude. Best of all I have discovered a gorge, sloping gently on one side, the other a huge boulder covered with moss; in the bottom of the gorge a brook pushing its tortuous way over rocks; and alders and ferns close to the banks. Overhead there is a rift of sky, and the sunlight flickers about generously, and the woods I have come through look so dark and impenetrable. There is a fine dry rock with the alders meeting like an arbour above it, and I sit there by the hour and wonder why the forest ever made me feel over-civilised. Beside these people I feel a pure child of Nature. They have reached a pitch of correctness I never can hope to attain. They never use slang, they punctuate their sentences so beautifully, they would not drop a final g in our careless fashion for worlds; they pronounce all their syllables so distinctly! Oh, this is "culture," Polly mine. If poor dear Matthew Arnold could only come back and live among them! Perhaps he does in spirit and that is his idea of Heaven. (It would be mine of Hell). And we have so misjudged the Americans, believing them to be crass and exaggerated. I assure you there is nothing exaggerated about the true aristocrats except their virtues; those are superlative, but in all other things they aim at simple perfection only, and from their enunciation to their boots—they have the dearest little feet—I can tell you, Polly, they have attained it. I feel so crude—

and so happy. I come out here to my brook—I am writing to you with its baby roar and lap in my ears—and I say all sorts of dreadful things quite loud. I forget that I ever have sizzled in London drawing-rooms, proud and happy in my court and interested in nothing in life but gowns and conquests. I forget the whole atmosphere of flirtation and intrigue and gay recklessness and heartbreak. I can tell you, Polly, that when you have stood as close to death as I have done during the last two years, with your heart-strings on the rack and the tears never far from your eyes, you are well prepared to retreat into the arms of Nature and cower there. I have no desire left to return to the world, and if Bertie can live comfortably here I should be glad and happy to remain for an indefinite number of years. My prince can find me here as well as anywhere. He is not Mr. Rogers, charming as he is. He never could stir up my great emotions—and I have them! I wonder if these people ever have suffered as I have, or if they ever have loved passionately? I cannot imagine it. They are too well-regulated, and that discontent which gently agitates them is merely the result of living in a country where nothing is unattainable, and, consequently, where ambition never sleeps, even when it takes no form.

I have met most of the men now and like some of them rather well. At least they talk less than the women and do not seem to fancy themselves so much. They are quite content to be just men and do the sensible things every-day men usually do without bothering about it. They say much prettier things to one than our men do, and I like it, but how much they mean I am not prepared to say. They are not in the least exaggerated or silly in their admiration, like a Frenchman or a Spaniard —will you ever forget that experience in Madrid? —for their common sense and their sense of humour never fail them. And they are all clever—no doubt of that!—but somehow their cleverness does not annoy one as the women's does. Perhaps it is because they have not had time for the excessive "culture" of the women. Mr. Hammond, for instance, has not attempted to read everything in every language ever written, but he can talk sensibly about most things, particularly the affairs of the world. Mr. Chenoweth leaves Mrs. Chenoweth to blow his horn, and never mentions "shop;" but he does look so dyspeptic, poor man, and he has not Mr. Hammond's pleasant air of repose. He likes to play with his children, however, and I love him for that.

Then there is an "author" who writes the poorest short stories I ever read—I have only a magazine knowledge of his work—but he belongs to the "set." Mr. Chenoweth is his intimate friend and his wealth enables him to give his chosen circle such entertainment as quite reconciles them to the poverty of his literary dower. Still, I cannot quite see why the public should be inflicted with him. He is quite bright to talk to, a very agreeable dinner companion, I fancy. I should like him rather if he were more honest with himself—and did not make epigrams.

Take them all in all they are as distinguished-looking—or should I have said "refined?"—as they feel it their duty to be, and quite as agreeable as I would have them—which is more to the point.

There is a Mr. Nugent, a guest, at the Club House, of Mr. Rogers, who rather interests me the most. I think on the whole I must tell you a little experience. He is about forty and a "brilliantly successful" lawyer. He has argued famous cases before the Supreme Court, amassed a fortune, and his admirers—not this set—want him to go into politics. He is very striking in appearance, tall, thin, nervous, with a lean, clever, hard, mobile face, an eye that burns and penetrates, a mouth that looks as if it had conquered everything but his passions, and a quick nervous grip of the hand which suggests that what he does he does quickly and wastes no time arguing about. Next to Mr. Rogers Bertie likes him better than anyone up here, and I must confess he rather fascinates me. I am wicked enough to want to see a man like that go off his head about me. But I fancy I'd have my hands full if he ever did let go. Mr. Rogers—he is getting rather devoted, my dear—I always could manage, because he would be so afraid of making himself ridiculous that he hardly would allow his voice to tremble unless I almost proposed to him. He burst out one day: "You white English rose!" I fear I used my eyelashes rather wickedly, and my upper lip, for he drew a step nearer and the colour came into his grey face. Then I felt my eyes twinkle and he recovered himself in a manner that would have done credit to a woman-of-the-world in her fourteenth flirtation; men are usually so clumsy about these things; he smiled quickly and added in the light tone of any man complimenting any woman: "You are really unique here, you know, Lady Helen. Perhaps lily is rather your prototype in the floral world than rose. You make my countrywomen seem like hot-house flowers—if there were a floral heaven they would all be beautiful orchids in the next world.

But to return to Mr. Nugent. One warm evening when he was calling on us and we were sitting on the piazza I asked him if he intended to go into politics. It is very difficult to make him talk of anything consecutively, by the way, and that makes him resemble us in one particular, at least. There are no semi-colons in *his* conversation, mostly dashes.

"I have not made up my mind, Lady Helen. It is an alluring prospect in one way, but I should be obliged to give up—those are wonderful clouds."

They were, Polly. Above the mountain behind the Club House were two enormous masses of cloud that looked like colossal blue dishes piled to the heavens with whipped cream. They were almost alike and you cannot imagine anything more perfect than that cream whipped into form by a giant hand. I thought out loud and Mr. Nugent said hastily:

"Oh, call it sea foam, not cream."

"But sea foam looks like yeast," I objected. "I don't think you are a bit more poetical than I am."

He laughed heartily (these Americans can flatter so with their laugh). "I am quite discomfited," he said, "and I can only add that I have far more reason to be poetical than yourself."

"Very neat," said Bertie. I can imagine my beloved brother thinking it worth while to say the charming things these men do.

"Now tell me some more of your politics," I persisted. "Mr. Rogers thinks politics are not respectable, but if the stables can be cleaned in one country they can in another."

"Exactly, but if I went in for cleaning, in other words for reform—I should sacrifice a great deal. I am lawyer for one of the greatest Trusts in the United States, and as I could not consistently as a reformer—in the present exaggerated state of public opinion—remain in such a position,—that would mean the sacrifice of a large slice of my income."

"I must say I admire your frankness, but *how* can you be counsel for a Trust?"

"Why not?—so long as I have not taken a stand."

"How can an honest lawyer work for dishonest men?"

"The word dishonest, dear Lady Helen, is usually applied to Trusts by men who are not in them. Trusts are an evolution, nothing more, a combination effected that some may live rather than that all shall die. I am not going into sordid details, but I will add that the question never arose that did not have two sides, and that one side is as entitled to able legal counsel as the other. There is no reason in the world why this particular Trust, which is open and above board, should not have the best it can pay for, and as it has done me the honour to select me, I in return have given it the very best of my ability—which should salve any conscience. I feel the same way when defending a man against the combined prejudices of the community. He is entitled to the best defence he can command, and being a human being, is as worthy of it as his more approved opponent."

This was the longest speech I had ever heard him make, and I understood it as a defence of himself out of deference to me. So, I smiled at him in appreciation of the compliment, but replied:

"Still, I don't see why you value the money more than the public honour you might win."

"Money is a very good thing, Lady Helen, to a man with expensive tastes and a passion for travelling. If I went into politics I should not touch its money bags, for political money is invariably dirty; moreover, I should be obliged to sacrifice more or less of my general practice—and the result would be that I should be a comparatively poor man once more."

"Are you self-made?" I asked eagerly.

Once more he laughed heartily, and his remarkable eyes expressed that I might say anything I chose.

"In a way, yes, in another, no. My father was a prominent lawyer, but given to speculation in Wall Street.—He left little or nothing—I went into his office as soon as I left college—and although I was helped in the beginning I have made my own way—Ah! we are going to have a thunder-storm. Not in our whipped cream. That has been eaten by the gods. This cloud is full of energy and would interfere with the most immortal digestion. May I sit it out, or must I run?"

"Stay," said Bertie quickly, "I can't sleep in that infernal racket. Have some Scotch whiskey? Do you take it neat, or with soda? Nell, ring the bell, that's a good girl."

They refreshed themselves, and then we concluded to watch the storm till the rain came. The great cloud was a long time approaching and the thunder only a distant angry rumble. But the lightning? It never seemed to play on the surface, but leapt constantly from the deep caverns of the purple cloud, flashing into relief tortuous convolutions that looked heavy and flat when the fire played elsewhere. Sometimes it was only that volcanic flame, at other times the cloud seemed torn asunder, and down the rift ran the zig-zag thunder bolt. Now and again the forked lightning assumed strange shapes, like the fiery skeleton of a man's hand or of a gigantic leaf. Sometimes it leaped from peak to peak of that moving mountain, then suddenly darted hissing down a gorge as if in search of prey. What nervous impatient terrible energy, and what a tyrannical perversion of beauty!

I suddenly became aware that Mr. Nugent was watching me instead of the storm, and as I felt embarrassed I told him hurriedly what I had been thinking. Bertie had gone inside, as the lightning hurt his eyes.

"In a way that thunder cloud reminds me of you," I added, rather naughtily. "I don't mean that you are beautiful, but you seem full of that same nervous energy and you suggest that you might direct it rather cruelly."

"I don't think I should strike at random," he replied, still with his eyes on my face. "And at present I am in far more danger of being hit first."

It seemed to me that I felt something vibrate. Perhaps it was only the electricity in the air. At all events, I replied as placidly as if my breath had not shortened. "One of the rules of prize-fighting is to strike first, and the weaker should always keep that in mind, don't you think so?"

"Will you kindly tell me whom you consider the weaker?"

"Well—the woman—naturally."

"I should sleep much easier if I thought you did not know your power."

"Oh, sometimes my sex——"

"I am not talking of your sex but yourself."

The lightning flashed just then and I saw

more than his eyes. His whole face was eager and set. I could not help going a little further.

"I used to fancy I had some power over men —at least a good many seemed to love me—but during the last two years I have got out of practice rather. Positively I have not had the tiniest flirtation."

"No wonder you are so distractingly complete —I am afraid your life has been a sad one these two years," he added hurriedly, and, actually, his nervous peremptory voice softened. "Tell me something of it—But—pardon me—let me lift your shawl. The wind is coming and it will be very strong." He folded the shawl about me, and at the same time I heard Agatha reading to Bertie so I felt off duty for the present. And, Polly, I actually talked to him as I never talked to any but the oldest and dearest friend before. But he drew it out of me. I could no more resist that determined concentrated force beside me in the dark than I could push the electric carnival over the mountain. The man seemed magnetism incarnate, and every time the lightning flashed across his face I could see that sympathy which comes not from a soft heart but an intense personal interest. But perhaps that interest is the most highly prized of all by women, and whatever the mainspring, it was sweet to me, after all these months or terrible anxiety and suffering. I never talk things over with Agatha; I have avoided exchanging a glance of alarm with her; that would be too dreadful; and until now I never have felt sufficiently free from care to become interested enough in anyone for confidences. But —and I am not the least bit in love with him, Polly—I felt that I could talk to this man all night. The thunder cloud moved down the lake, carrying its rain with it, and I sat there for an hour and talked to him, while Bertie slept on a sofa just beyond the open window and Agatha read on.

"I don't think you like listening," I said breaking off abruptly. "I don't believe you ever listened so long to any one before."

"That is quite true. I am not a patient man and I am usually thinking about several things at once—But—I am not going to pay you any idle compliments. I will only say that I have great powers of realisation and that I have absolutely understood all you have felt and suffered during the last two years. I have felt it all so keenly that I wish I could do something to help you. I *am* going to be your friend," he added in his quick peremptory tones. "I will be your best friend in this country which must be so strange to you. I don't care a hang about Rogers' rights of priority. He isn't capable of understanding you as I do."

He took my hand suddenly in his warm magnetic clasp, and I had an odd feeling that he never intended to let it go. "This is only by way of pledging friendship," he said. "I am not going to disturb you by making love to you—not yet. I make no promises for the future. You have roused and bewildered and enthralled me. Whether it is love or not I don't know. Nor do I know what I can rouse in you. There is heaven and madness for some man. I am sure of that—but I —well, let all that go for the present. In the mean time I am your friend, remember that, and Rogers is to take a back seat."

I will admit, Polly, that I lay awake a long time that night thinking of him and reliving that peculiar sense of being encircled with warm magnetism. After all, I suppose that what we women want more than anything else is sympathy and a feeling of belonging to some one exclusively. And when a man has the passion to stir and warm and blind us how easily we can persuade ourselves that we are in love. But the *grande passion*—that is another thing. Of course you are in the throes of that and I rather envy you. Good night.

HELEN

Letter VI

From the Lady HELEN POLE *to the Countess of* EDGE *and* ROSS.

Boulder Lake,
July 17th

Dear Polly:

THIS afternoon I went over to Mrs. Laurence's "camp" for tea. She wrote me the most graceful little note with two witticisms in it, and as I had no excuse to offer, I went. Agatha and Bertie were also invited but A. had a headache and B. went fishing, saying the most uncomplimentary things about teas. Mr. Rogers and Mr. Nugent, who went with him, attempted no defence.

Mrs. Laurence has quite the most attractive camp. It is exactly like a doll's house, tiny but perfect, with two verandas, and it is full of dainty crétonnes and frills and bric-à-brac that no one could have selected but herself. She writes every morning in a doll's study, fitted up much like a boudoir, in blue the exact shade of her eyes; but in the afternoon she is always rustling about, and you hear her petulant voice and swishing skirts, with only short intervals of relief till bed-time.

She received us in a little clearing between the leafy maples on the right of her camp, and wore the most fetching gown of grass green lawn with a flopping white leghorn trimmed with green feathers. The others were all in the most charming white and flowered muslins and I was glad I had put on a soft white mull myself—Henriette has made me some charming hot weather frocks since we came—and by chance I too have a white leghorn, which I wore. It was trimmed with blue flowers, and my frock with blue ribbons. I did not look as original as Mrs. Laurence but—now I am going to say something nasty—I can stand a strong light and she cannot. To tell you the truth most of these women look rather passée in the sun. Their skins are so very thin and delicate that they line quickly, and so many of them have grey in their hair. However, they made a very charming picture under the trees and I must say for them that they appear to get on together delightfully.

They all greeted me with the utmost cordiality, but Mrs. Laurence rose from behind the tea table and offered me her cold hand with rather a forced smile.

"Please forgive me, dear Lady Helen, if I am thoroughly unamiable for a few moments," she pouted. "But I have been *so* annoyed." She swept her hand dramatically in the direction of a newspaper which evidently had been flung into the bushes. I recognised the New York ——.* "*That* has a picture of me, a large libellous photograph, procured, heaven knows how, certainly not from a friend! *Why* should they use my picture? *Why* should they mention my name? What possible interest can their readers—their million vulgar sensational readers—take in *me?* I don't suppose they ever heard my name before. It *is* hard when you have striven to belong to the aristocracy of letters to be flung into a cowshed."

I could not resist the temptation, although I trembled at my temerity: "I read the ——* every morning," I said. "Now, had I not met you, I should have been quite keen on seeing your picture."

* Deletions by the publisher.

"How sweet of you—but—Lady Helen—you don't read the ——.* You surely don't take it?"

I nodded, perfectly delighted at the twelve expressions of shocked amazement. "How is a stranger to master all your subtle distinctions at once? It seems to me very jolly and interesting. My brother is quite devoted to it."

"Well, I don't suppose it will do you any actual harm," said Mrs. Hammond, with an anxious expression, "but I assure you that if you were an American you never would admit that you read it—would not, indeed, have the least desire to read it—and I should really rejoice if you would reprove them by writing and withdrawing your subscription."

"Oh, I couldn't think of doing that," I said lightly. "My brother and I are studying your country, and you have nothing more representative."

"Representative?" Those carefully modulated voices were quite shrill.

*Deletion by the publisher.

I was in misery and my knees were shaking, but I determined to stand my ground.

"Do not you call a newspaper that a million people read every day, representative?" I answered. "What is it if not representative?"

"Of a certain class—yes," said Mrs. Chenoweth disgustedly. "But what a class!"

"A million people are not to be despised anywhere." I longed to ask Mrs. Laurence if she would prohibit—if she could—the ——'s * million readers from buying her books, but I didn't dare. I changed the subject instead by asking for a cup of tea.

But that conversation was nothing to one I took part in later.

I have not told you of Miss Shephard, for she did not come up with the others. She is the editor of a literary monthly magazine, issued by Mr. Rogers' publishing house. It is charmingly got up and quite a smart readable affair, but, Bertie and I had agreed, rather light and vague in criticism—although very pretentious—as compared

* Deletion by the publisher.

with our literary weeklies; in fact, not to be taken seriously as criticism at all. The half dozen numbers Mr. Rogers sent us left no impression on my mind whatever beyond a great many pages of clever writing by people who fancied their own opinions mightily. But when Mrs. Hammond told me that Miss Shephard was expected, she added that she was the brilliant editor of The ——, * and that probably no one living had a more exact knowledge of what constituted literature, including matter, form, style and perfect English than Miss Shephard. I cannot say that I was very keen to meet her, I am so tired of perfection, but when I saw her I was rather interested, for she does not appear to be more than one—or two-and-thirty. When I expressed some surprise at the position accorded her, I was assured that she had "genius" for criticism, and had, moreover, enjoyed the rare advantage of being the daughter of a Harvard professor and scholar who had been intimate with all the great literary lights of his time. She is a tall thin girl

* Deletion by the publisher.

with dark hair, mal coiffée, thoughtful grey eyes, a *very* refined nose and a thin ascetic mouth. Her skin looks worn, and there is an affected—so it strikes me—severity about her dress. But she has a thin sweet voice, and a very nice, if too serene, manner.

She did not sit near me during the tea, which was quite lively. Mrs. Laurence was brilliant as usual and moved about a good deal, particularly after Mr. Rolfs "dropped in" unexpectedly and some of his admirers showed a disposition to hang upon the words which a large piece of cake made even more weighty. Finally he did talk—to make her more jealous, I think—and gave them quite a lecture on celestial botany, as it were. Mrs. Laurence could only get the better of him by capping his melodious paragraphs with scintillating epigrams, which annoyed him excessively. I sincerely wish they would murder each other. Finally I became so bored that I wandered down to the edge of the lake, and in a moment Miss Shephard joined me.

"Like all great writers," she said apologetically, "he puts his best in his books, and sometimes lacks magnetism and fresh thought in talking."

For some reason Miss S. antagonises me. Perhaps it is a certain air of omniscience, the result of being a factor in the destinies of so many great and brilliant authors. So I answered with some pleasure:

"I think Mr. Rolfs' books as dull as his speech. He has his points, but he is not a *born* author, therefore you see the little glittering implements and smell the oil all the time, and of course his stories do not *go*."

"There is some truth in what you say," she answered sweetly, "but then don't you think that a man with so great and beautiful a mind should be above being a good story-teller?"

"Shakespeare was not."

"True, dear Lady Helen, but I need not remind you that we are in neither the times nor the country of Shakespeare. Have you observed how non-imitative, how independent we are? There was a time, of course, when American writers slavishly imitated, and in consequence burlesqued, English literature; the only exceptions were Hawthorne and Poe, and, later, Mark Twain and Bret Harte; but the literature of the last twenty years, which includes so many illustrious names—surely there never has been anything like it in the world."

"There never has! I suppose I am old-fashioned but it wearies and irritates me—I do not wish to be rude—but—really—I like to read about men and women with human passions."

"Oh, a discussion without frankness is a poor affair. I am sure that yours is merely a first impression and that our literature will fascinate you in time. Will you permit me a brief explanation? It is our object to produce a literature which shall demonstrate in what ways we are different from all other nations—those differences, peculiarities and so forth which our new and in all things unique country has evolved. Why should we demonstrate—and encourage—the worn out passions that are common to all countries? The refined of ours prefer to forget that such things exist. All well-brought up American girls are taught to ignore this lamentable side of human nature, and never voluntarily to think of it. Without boasting I think I can say that this is the most *refined* country the world has ever known, and that our literature proves it."

"But occasionally you develop an author of irrepressible virility who gives the world to understand that a certain percentage at least of the United States are very much like the old accepted idea of human nature."

"They do not count," she said emphatically, "because we will not admit them to the ranks of literature, and they *must* go to the wall in time. The literary pages of the high-class newspapers, and the weekly and monthly bulletins never paragraph them, never refer to them, except in the reviews which advertising exigencies compel. Then we kill them by sneers, not abuse—which always excites a lamentable current in human nature. They are quietly brushed aside, and the real jewels of American literature forced into even greater prominence."

"Suppose one of these outsiders equals the elect in literary quality?"

"He cannot, because matter and manner are really one. They are too *strong*, too bold and unpleasant, therefore they shatter and deface that fine exquisite thing called style."

"Your style. Cannot you conceive the possibility of any other standard being as correct?"

"Certainly not. It is a subject to which we have given years of earnest and analytical thought."

"What of the very different standards of England, France, Germany, Russia? The novels of all countries seem to be issued by your American firms—and, presumably, read."

"Oh, we are quite willing that each country should have its own standard. Those old states, indeed, could not imitate us, for they have not the same material. Therefore when a successful European novel treats of things that no well-bred American will discuss, we are generous enough not to be hyper-critical of a race which differs from us in every particular. The older nations are naturally coarse, and allowance should be made for them. But there is not one of our elected authors who would dare or care to treat a subject in the same way. And why *should* he deal with nasty passion? He has the brilliant kaleidoscopic surface of American life to treat."

"And you cannot conceive of a day when the standard will change?"

"Certainly not."

"The minority of one generation is usually the majority of the next," I said, now warmed to the theme. "Your people of the world—and I know that you have that class—have chosen as their favourites the very authors you have tabooed, and whose works do not reach, I am told, the great public you instruct. As these few authors set their faces against emasculation they offend your aristocratic middle-class, and as they are not erotic your unspeakable sub-stratum will have none of them; but they deal truthfully with that world which those of your country who have enjoyed superior advantages can stand reading about."

I had hit her at last. She coloured and drew

herself up. " I do not understand your term 'aristocratic middle-class,' " she said icily. " And I can only assert definitely that we who give our brains and time and culture to the subject are setting and maintaining a standard that always will prevail."

I turned to go and say good-bye to Mrs. Laurence, but I could not forbear a parting shot. I waved my hand at the company.

" I wonder they marry," I said. " And I think it positively indecent of them to have children."

20th July

I am very much alone these days. Bertie is so much better that he spends the entire day fishing or at the Club House, and frequently dines and spends the evening there as well. Agatha has discovered at least twenty neglected correspondents and writes as hard as Mrs. Laurence or Mr. Rolfs, all the morning. I do not mind that, for it keeps her in the house and I can receive any of the men who care to call; but *every* afternoon, Polly, she goes to Mrs. Chenoweth's and plays whist, and I either have to shut myself up like a nun or walk in the woods alone. Of course I could defy the dear old soul, but that would be the end of an ideal domestic harmony, and as for Bertie he would be furious. Mr. Rogers is the only person privileged to walk alone with me, and I do not know whether he is flattered or not. I had heard a good deal about the liberty of American girls, but Mrs. Chenoweth assures me that that is all a mistake as far as the upper classes are concerned. Still, I have had a good many conversations with Mr. Nugent, and some day perhaps I'll relate them to you. He calls in the evening and we wander off the veranda to the edge of the lake and stand there for an hour or so admiring the sunset, and once or twice we have met quite accidentally in the forest. After all, I do not own the trail down the mountain even if it is my favourite one. He certainly is interesting, Polly, although in so different a way from all the men I have ever known or read about that I really do not know whether I like him or not. He fascinates me, but that is his magnetism, the concentration of his preternaturally clever mind upon myself, the brilliant and unexpected things he says, and the truly delightful little attentions he pays me, when I know that he is full of restlessness and hardness, and ambition and nervous contempt of the details of life. But the moment he comes near me I feel protected and surrounded; I am possessed immediately to drop my shawl or handkerchief or worry about the punkies—dreadful little beasts that he keeps off very effectively with a fan or his hat. Once I made him go down on his knees and tie my shoe, merely because I wanted him to see that my foot was as small as any of his countrywomen's, in spite of my five ft. seven, and much better shod. On another day I had a headache, and instead of remaining in bed I had Henriette arrange me luxuriously on a divan in the living-room, and received him when he called. I had an uncontrollable desire to see how he would act when I was ill. He was charming, in an abrupt, sincere, and wholly tactless way. I think if I had known others like him or had known him about five years I should almost fall in love with him; but how we cling to our ideals! Independence of thought! We are all creatures of traditions.

I may just as well tell you first as last, Polly, that I am sure both Mr. Rogers and Mr. Nugent have made up their minds to marry me. Agatha is blind and Bertie amused, for he cannot imagine me falling in love with anything un-English and new. You see, I *look* so—well, traditional, few know or suspect that I am impetuous and full of curiosity and love of novelty *inside*. Of course, as I said, I am in a way as traditional as I look, but in another I'm not. I don't know if I have expressed myself clearly.

I am sure that Mr. Rogers and all of them think that he has the better chance, because he is so cold and calm and correct. He really is charming in his way and I think I might have had rather a jolly little flirtation with him if Mr. Nugent had not happened to be a guest of the Club. But *he* talks to me about things that interest me so much more, and he has made me talk to him about myself as I never talked before—even to you. If I could remember all of the nonsense we have talked I'd write it to you, but you know I never did have any memory.

The other day a year-old doe mysteriously appeared in our ice-house with my name printed on a card lying on its chest. I *know* that either Mr. R. or Mr. N. shot it for me, but I do not dare thank one or the other or even hint the subject: the game laws are so severe that it would be like a breach of confidence. But it has made all other meat insipid and we enjoyed it quite enough to compensate the offender for the risk he ran. It was one evening when both were calling that I regretted being obliged to wait till September for the game I like best.

Mr. N's first name is Luke.

22nd July

Well, I will tell you of one conversation at least between Mr. Nugent and myself. A very celebrated—you may be sure he is in the superlative class—lung specialist came up the other day to visit the Chenoweths. Although Bertie is apparently so much better, the moment this doctor appeared I felt that I must have a verdict. At first I thought of appealing to Mr. Rogers, but finally concluded that as I had talked so much to Mr. Nugent it would be positively unkind to pass him over; besides it is so much easier to speak to him about *anything*. The *one* thing that keeps me from feeling the *perfect* freedom of friendship when I am alone with him is the fear that he suddenly will lose his head and take me in his arms and kiss me. He looks passion incarnate and I know that if he ever did let go he would be like one of these alarming electrical storms that visit us every two or three days. However, I have managed him rather well, so far.

Well, I confided in him, and he engaged to persuade Dr. Soulé and Bertie to meet for examination, and pledged himself to get the truth out of the doctor and tell me every word of it. It was finally agreed—Bertie was a long time being persuaded—that they were to meet this morning in Mr. Nugent's room and that at four this afternoon Mr. N. and I would meet at a certain spot in the forest, where I should hear the fateful truth—I thought the appointment was justifiable in the circumstances.

By three I was so nervous that I could not stay in the house and I plunged into the forest, praying that I would meet no one else. Fortunately our camp is alone on our side of the lake and the others prefer the trails behind the Club House and at the north end. I walked far down the mountain to quiet my nerves a little, then returned to the place where we had agreed to meet. It was the rocky brook I told you of, but some distance below the boulder. The opposite bank sloped up gently, its gloom hung with scattered leaves and sun-flecks. I sat down on a rock among the alders, still nervous, my hand, indeed, pressed against my heart, but—what strange tricks the mind plays us—my terrible anxiety crossed by imaginings of what Mr. N. would do and say should he bring me the worst. In a moment, too, my mind was diverted by the dearest sight. A chipmunk—a tiny thing no longer than my finger with a snow white breast and reddish brown back striped with grey and ivory—sat on his hind legs on a stone opposite me eating a nut which he held in his front paws. His black restless eyes never left my face as he tore that nut apart with teeth and nail, and he seemed to have made up his little mind that I was quite stationary—he did seem to enjoy that nut so much. His bushy tail stood straight up behind and curled back from his head. It was quite an inch longer than himself, and not a bit of him moved but those tight little arms and those crunching teeth. He ate the entire nut, and when he had finished and dropped the shell, he still sat there on his hind legs, glancing about, his eyes never wandering far from my face, and absorbing my attention so completely that I quite forgot the apprehension that had torn me for the past four hours. But our mutual interest was shattered by a footstep. I sprang to my feet and he scampered into the ferns.

The moment I saw Mr. N.'s face I knew that I was not to hear the worst, at all events; and then, for the life of me, I could not let the subject be broached. I hurriedly commenced to tell him about the chipmunk and he sat down on the stone it had deserted and listened as if he never had heard of a chipmunk before.

"I'll try and get you one," he said. "I think one might be tamed."

"Oh, I should love it!" I exclaimed. "It would be company for hours at a time. I am sure it has intelligence."

"I am afraid you have many lonely hours," he said. "I think you do not like our people here."

"No," I said, "they fidget me. I really admire them and I never in all my life believed that so many clever people could be got together in one place. But—that is it—they are not my own sort."

"No, they are not, and I have a plan to propose to you, that I think might be carried out now that your brother is so much better. I have a number of friends at another lake about ten miles from here. They are very different from these—far more like what you have been used to. They belong to one of the worldly sets in New York, and, while they are quite as clever as our friends here, cleverness is not their métier and they are not so self-conscious about it. They bought Chipmunk Lake and built cottages there that they might go into camp whenever they felt that they needed rest more than Europe or Newport—Should you like to visit there ?"

"Yes, but how ?"

"I should have said that my married sister is there and that I have written to her about you. She would be delighted if you would pay her a visit. Of course Lady Agatha will go with you, and the Duke can transfer himself to the Club House for a time."

"He is there always, anyhow," I said, and I suspect I pouted. At all events he smiled sympathetically and said,

"I am afraid you have learned already something of the selfishness and ingratitude of man."

"It is a good preparation for matrimony," I remarked drily.

"Are you contemplating matrimony ?" It is interesting rather to bring some colour into the face of an American.

"I am always afraid I might marry some time when I am unusually bored."

"It is not so great a risk to bore you, then?"

"Oh, I mean by Circumstances. I should expect the man to descend suddenly into them with the wings of an archangel and bear me off."

"Are you very much bored here? Have I come too soon?"

"I never have enjoyed myself so much."

"Nevertheless you are not averse to a change."

"Oh, as my time is short in the United States and as human nature is the most interesting study in the world, I want to meet as many of your interesting types as possible."

"Your stay may be longer than you think. Soulé says that the Duke must not think of leaving the Adirondacks for two years."

He had me at last. "Two years!" I gasped. "Must we stay up here for two years?" The place has lost some of its charm since these people came.

"Not here, for you would be snowed in in winter and uncomfortable in every way. I have suggested to the Duke that he endeavour at once to lease a house at Lake Placid. There you would be close to an express train to New York—which you could visit frequently — and undoubtedly could find a house with golf links, tennis court, etc., to say nothing of good trails where you could have daily rides. I know you are longing to be on a horse again."

"Oh, I am! How did you guess it? That does not sound so hopeless. I suppose our friends would visit us occasionally."

"I can assert positively that some of them would come as often as they were asked."

"It would be charity, of course. How kind you and Mr. Rogers have been to think of everything for us."

Again I had managed to bring the colour into his face. "Rogers is a kind fatherly soul," he said, tartly. "I don't pretend to be philanthropic."

Here I was afraid he would propose to me so I said hurriedly:

"We have forgotten all about Chipmunk Lake. I should like to see some other lakes and some other people. But it is a great deal to ask of your sister."

"My sister is undoubtedly pining for a new

acquaintance. There are only four families at the lake and they soon get talked out. Will you go? I may as well confess that I have already written to and heard from her. Here is her note to you."

It was such a jolly letter, so direct and natural and unwitty. I felt at home with her at once—her name is Mrs. Van Worden, and I liked her further because she spelt Van with a capital V. I am told that Van in New York is quite an insignia of nobility and I met two of its proud possessors in London who had it printed on their cards with a small v. Considering that it is over every other shop in Holland and Belgium, this certainly is an instance of American progressiveness.

But to return to Mr. Nugent—who is delightfully free of all nonsense, bless him.

"Yes, I do want to go," I said, "and I hope it can be arranged—if only for the pleasure of meeting Mrs. Van Worden. I *feel* I shall get on with her."

"Yes, you will get on, I am sure. She and

her friends at the lake belong to the great world without going in for *all* its frivolities and vulgarities. Let us go back and arrange it at once," he said, jumping up. "There is no reason why we should not go to-morrow."

24th

But we did not go "to-morrow," Polly, and I have not been really hopeful of going until to-night. Agatha said quietly and impassively that, better or not, nothing would induce her to leave Bertie, that she would never sleep three yards away from him until he was quite well again. That left me without a chaperon, for although Mrs. Van Worden had written her a charming note too, she had not invited anyone else at the lake, and I believe she knows several of them. Whether this omission rankled—she appears to be quite a personage—or whether they are all determined I shall marry Mr. Rogers, I don't know, but I was invited to the Club House to luncheon next day and not less than four women attempted to dissuade me from going. The road was "frightful," quite the worst in the Adirondacks. Life there was unbearably dull. They were worked out society women who took a sort of rest cure in the Adirondacks, eating and sleeping themselves into a condition of recuperating stupidity. There were "no men," as the fishing was not good, and too many other drawbacks to mention. It was Mrs. Hammond who was commissioned with the final dissuasions. She walked home with me, and as we were crossing the pretty rustic bridge over the lake's outlet, she put her hand in my arm, and said with a slight blush:

"You must not mind what I am going to say to you, dear Lady Helen, I take such an interest in you. Who could help it?—you are so beautiful and a stranger here. And of course I am nearly ten years older than yourself and a married woman. I *don't* want you to go to those people; they are all rather fast. Mrs. Van Worden has had several stories in circulation about her that have come very close to being scandals——."

"What!" I cried, "am I really to meet an

American woman who has committed adultery? How much at home I shall feel! So many of my friends have, you know."

"Lady Helen!" Never shall I forget that gasping shriek nor that poor scandalized little face. I almost relented.

"If she will only admit it," I pursued gloomily, "but they scarcely ever will. I do know one American woman who told me the second time I met her that she had a lover, but she had lived in England fifteen years and cut all her American acquaintances. I cannot understand your reticence."

"Lady Helen! Do you mean to insinuate that any of us——"

"Oh, dear me, no. You are all shockingly virtuous here."

She stared at me for a moment longer, then curiosity got the better of her horror. She did not replace her hand within my arm, but she resumed her walk to my camp, evidently determined to understand me.

"Let us have this out, Lady Helen, I implore

you?" she said. "Do I understand that you countenance immorality?"

"I accept the inevitable. It does not appeal to me personally, but if it does to other women and helps them to dissipate the ennui of life, that is none of my affair."

"Ah, that is the result of having every good thing in life flung at your feet, of living an idle life of fashion that has no excitement left in it but intrigue."

"Our lowest class is much worse than our highest, and quite open and unembarrassed about it."

"I cannot account for it!" The poor little woman's voice was tragic.

"Why try to account for everything? Facts are facts, that is enough."

"I never have really believed one tenth of the scandals of fashionable life I have heard—I have trained myself to wait for divorce-court proof——"

"You have tried to dissuade me from visiting Mrs. Van Worden because she is suspected of having loved more frequently than she has married."

"Oh, but that does not mean that I *believe* it. I simply do not want you to be identified with a woman who has been talked about. She certainly cannot contaminate you if you hold such extraordinary views. But *do* you, dear Lady Helen?"

"Yes," I said impatiently. "Don't you? Do you pretend to ignore the fact that hundreds of thousands of women have lovers."

"I *will* not admit it."

"But you know it if you know anything at all. Like your literature you blink it, as you blink every other fact connected with real life."

Again she stopped and stared at me. "You look the incarnation of maiden purity," she exclaimed, "a tall white royal English lily, as Mr. Rogers calls you. It seems incredible that you can have such a perverted mind. You remind me of that dreadful heroine of Mallock's—— "

"I have not a perverted mind," I exclaimed angrily, for she really was too silly, "and I have nothing in common with that filthy creature——"

"I beg your pardon," she interrupted hurriedly, "no one on earth would ever accuse *you* of being less stainless—really—than you look—I mean your mind—your knowledge——Oh," she continued desperately, "I can't make you out. I have heard of the insolent frankness of the English aristocracy—that you hold yourself above all laws—the Duke is terrifyingly coarse at times—and I suppose if you had done anything wrong you wouldn't pay me the compliment to deny it—but —well—I give it up."

"My mind is not perverted," I said, "because I see life as it is. I have lived in the world now for eight years, and all my friends happen to have married long since. I should have been a fool had I not seen and heard what life meant to many people, even if I never had had any confidences made me. But it has not stained my mind in the least, because it is something I never think of when by myself—which is the result of accepting life and human nature as they are not as they ought to be. I will not pretend to say, however, that I do not sympathize with women who are carried away by passion. I do not see how a woman who has any passion ——"

"Lady Helen! I cannot let you go any further. I am willing to admit that there is sin in the world, but there are certain standards of refinement in this country that I will not hear violated."

"What on earth are you talking about?"

"I mean that—well—that I cannot listen to a woman admit that she has passions exactly like a man."

"Do you mean that you never heard that before?" I asked curiously.

"Never! There are certain obligations—but—Oh, don't let us talk of it. There is one thing further I feel I must say—and I am hoping you will pardon me, for we are all hoping and longing to keep you among us—you and dear Lady Agatha, although of course we know that we must lose the clever Duke when he is well enough to go home——"

She paused, and I gave her my most encouraging smile. We were on the veranda now and she sat opposite me, leaning forward alertly.

"It is this," she said with her anxious smile. "We all do so want you to marry our dear brilliant accomplished Mr. Rogers, and not Mr. Nugent. *He* is not really one of us, and, I am afraid he is not too high-principled and has not led an immaculate life—like Mr. Rogers."

"How can you tell?"

"By their faces. Look at Mr. Rogers'. It is refinement itself, almost ascetic. Mr. Nugent looks—well—of course he is a gentleman and irreproachable in society, but I *know* he has not led a regular life."

"I am sure he has not, and it is really none of our business."

"I believe that men should be as pure as women," she said setting her lips.

"Perhaps they should, but they are not; you see there are so many women who make a business of tempting them from the time they begin to take notice that it is quite unreasonable to expect them to attain the feminine standard."

"I am not talking of bad women."

"Oh, but they count so, you know. They count because they are the positive force. Virtue is too negative to influence anyone but those who are virtuous by nature or circumstance. But as I said before, dear Mrs. Hammond, facts are facts. Why not accept them, and without so much mental wear and tear? Every man has the privilege of leading his own life, so long as he keeps within the law. And if he does not think he is doing wrong, if he does not violate his conscience, then he does himself no moral harm so long as he sins like a gentleman. Of course no one wants the coarse sensualist near one; he is repulsive and should herd with his own kind."

"And you mean to say you extenuate—you would marry a man who had—who had—made love to many women? I am interested in your views, but I must reiterate that I think if social exigencies compel us to meet such men we should at least discourage their kind by refusing to marry them."

She looked pale and nervous but her eyes were bright with curiosity.

"I will tell you my theory," I said, "and I can assure you that I did not jump at it. As I told you, I have seen a good deal of the world, the best of it as well as some of its worst. This is my idea—But first: If God is incarnate in good men and the devil in bad why are bad men invariably more fascinating to women—even to pure women—than good men? I am talking of course of the devil which dwells in masculine and able men, not in the silly and ingenuous sensualist. Now the men who are wholly irresistible are those who combine both God and devil, who stimulate and intensify the soul and the imagination as well as the passions. This confounds orthodoxy, but does not to my mind deepen the mystery. Is not this combination, perhaps, the perfect man? And as man is—we believe—made in the divine image—may not God and the devil be one rounded being? Why does the 'perfect' man and woman invariably irritate and antagonize, even have a bad influence,—arousing the devil of perversity—when the perfection is in the least self-conscious? Is it not because we instinctively feel their failure to achieve the standard we have accepted as divine, and resent the imposition? And can such a one-sided being give happiness? Not any more than the lowest brute. Therefore, I maintain that a man to reach full stature must have room in his soul for God and the devil to jog along peacefully side by side."

She rose, white and aghast. "I never, never heard anything to approximate that for audacity —and—and—terrible profanity. But I am too nervous to argue with you. I see Mrs. Laurence coming. Please tell her—*she* is so brilliant, so gifted. I know she could refute——"

"Please tell her that I have not had a walk to-day! that I shall have a violent headache if I miss it! *Please* be an angel and don't tell her I saw her coming—" and I almost ran to the back veranda and plunged into the woods. I had screwed up my courage to the highest pitch and I knew I couldn't do it a second time. I felt nervous, almost excited, and I wanted a walk and the solitude of the woods.

I walked rapidly down the trail for ten or fifteen minutes, then felt a sudden desire to see that precipitous magnificent avenue made by the roadway. I entered it presently and walked down the logs as rapidly as I could, for the exercise; pausing whenever I reached a ledge—in these woods you cannot walk and admire at the same time unless you care to run the risk of a broken ankle—to drink in that wild yet awesome perspective of the forest. The trees are so high, and often their branches leap across and clasp hands!—and crowding upon the heels of the advance guard is the green, fragrant, ancient army, a million strong. And every now and again the distant mountain beyond the high wild valley.

I suddenly became possessed with a desire to get closer to that mountain, to get away from my own for a little while. I knew that it could not be more than four miles off, and I could easily make the distance and return before dark. I almost felt as if I were running away, and hurried on eagerly.

I passed Mr. Rolfs sitting cross-legged on a

damp boulder, communing—presumably—with God. There was a note-book beside him. He looked like an omniscient owl. As I passed he bowed gravely but did not speak. I am positive he cannot endure me.

I went down the mountain as rapidly as I could, but that is saying little. What between picking my way over logs that slipped and stones that cut and feeling for dry land through the grass by the roadside I was fully an hour reaching the valley. It was just a few moments before making the last precipitous descent, when I paused for a moment on a ledge and fanned myself, that I became aware how hot and sultry it was. Almost at the same moment I heard the loud familiar rumble of the approaching storm.

It would take me longer to reach home than it had done to pick my way down that beastly road. There was nothing to do but make for the valley and the nearest house, and the sudden brief copper of the sky made me hasten on with all speed. I do not experience any sinking physical fear during a thunder-storm but I have a mental appreciation of the danger and I prefer to be within four walls with the doors and windows closed. The storm was still far off, for the intervals between the flash and the clap were quite long, and its rain was deluging some other mountain miles away.

At last I was free of the woods and stood in the great valley with its irregular masses of mountains on every side, its rivers, its wide peaceful clearings, and alas! its cows. There was no building within a mile except a dilapidated Catholic church, the most mournful object I ever saw in a landscape. Half of the roof was gone, a thousand rains had washed its last coat of paint away, the fence was but a few broken sticks, and the grass and weeds grew high over three or four poor forgotten graves. There was a French colony about here, long since.

It was not an attractive refuge, but the great thunder-cloud was pushing its way across the Eastern mountain, forked and torn with fire, and roaring as if it were Hell moving up to Summer quarters.

I was therefore about to make for the ruin when I heard the sound of a sob and of running feet behind me. I turned quickly and saw, running toward me and wringing her hands, a slight pretty girl, with a mass of fluffy hair surmounted by an immense hat covered with blue feathers.

"Oh, please, wait for me," she cried. "I'm so skaret, and I've been runnin' roun' like I was crazy. Its a mile to the nearest farm and I dassent go in that spooky church by myself. Oh, my Gawd, ain't it awful."

"Why, there are thunder-storms nearly every day," I said soothingly. "There is really nothing to be afraid of. Let us go into the church, by all means."

I was glad of her company, to tell you the truth, and led the way rapidly to the ruin. The door was locked! but we picked our way to the back, past those desolate graves, and entered where a wall had fallen in. It was not an easy task to scramble over the mouldering remains of roof and wall, but we accomplished it and ensconced ourselves in a pew in that end of the structure which was still whole enough to afford shelter, although how much of safety was doubtful.

We were none too soon. Almost immediately the rain came down with that furious energy characteristic of storms in these mountains, the thunder was really appalling, and the lightning seemed to have got beyond control of itself—the forks cut its steady blaze. My companion had possessed herself of my hand and cowered against me. Her vernacular as exhibited in a disconnected monologue quite distracted my mind from the storm.

"Oh, my Gawd," she would mutter; then with a violent start: "Gee whizz! Wat for did I ever come up to these mountains and I alwus so afraid of lightnin'? O-w-w! Oh, Lordy I'll never do it agin, I vow I won't. Oh, Joc *why* ain't you here? I'm skaret plum to death. I know I'll be struck clean to kingdom come, and I ain't so bad. I really ain't. Oh, Joc you ain't treaten' me right to be safe down there in Noo York and me goin' to be kilt for ever up on these wicked mountins."

Fortunately, the electricity had other havoc to accomplish before its force was spent, and passed quickly, leaving only the rain behind it. She recovered herself almost as quickly and sat up and smoothed her hair, then took off her hat and regarded the feathers.

"They ain't wet, thank heavings," she said, then readjusted it carefully; after which she turned and regarded me with suspicion. She was a pretty dainty creature, not as common as you would expect, for the national delicacy of feature and sensitiveness of expression seem quite as impartial as democracy could demand.

"Who are you?" she asked. "I ain't seen you before in these parts."

"I am on the mountain, at Boulder Lake."

A light flashed into her damp eyes. "Aw, now, you ain't that there Lady Helen somethin', a dook's sister, what everybody is talkin' about?"

I bowed in as graceful acknowledgment as I could muster and she pursued delightedly:

"You look like it and I've seen a lord as didn't, but you look just like you might be the hero*ine* of a story in the 'Family Herald'."

"I have not the pleasure of the 'Family Herald's' acquaintance," I said, smiling genially, for she interested me as another variety of the genus American, "but tell me something of yourself. You are not a mountain girl, I infer."

"Cheese it!" she exclaimed scornfully. "Do I look like these here lumps that is as broad as they is long and wear their hair as slick as a rat's tail? Naw, I'm a Noo Yorker born and bred, and I'm a sales-lady in ——— * See?"

"You mean—a—shop girl?"

"Naw. We don't use that there kind of language in this country. This is the United States of Ameriky and we're all free and equal."

"Ah," I exclaimed eagerly. "Do *you* really hold to that? How refreshing. Then you don't look down on these mountain girls that usually have to work as servants?"

"Gee!" she exclaimed indignantly, "I guess I

* Deletion by the publisher.

do. Servants is one thing and sales-ladies is another. And I ain't never goin' to the mountins agin for vacations—not while there's cheap hotels at Asbury Park, and Ocean Grove. I ain't used to settin at table with servants, or 'hired help' as they call themselves. But a lady frien' of mine's got an aunt up here and she giv me no peace till I come, I was that near dead with work and heat."

If I were of an hysterical turn I probably should have succumbed. But I maintained a becoming gravity and looked at her with that concentrated interest which forces people to talk about themselves.

"But," I said diffidently,—"as you have told me you work you won't mind my alluding to it—suppose you had been less clever than you are or had had less influence than you did have—and had been forced to go out as a servant——"

"I'd 'a been a fluff first—naw, I don't mean that. But I just wasn't—that's all. And I guess I ain't goin' to associate with those beneath me when I don't have to. Wouldn't I be a fool if I did?"

"You certainly would not be a good American. But if you call yourself 'sales-lady' why should not the poor servant be permitted to ease her self-respect by calling herself 'hired help'?"

"She kin, for all of me, but it don't make her nothin' else. I hear somebody comin'"—her voice fell to a terrified whisper. "Oh, lordy, I hope it ain't a tramp."

It was Mr. Rogers. His anxious face appeared above the rubbish, and I spoke immediately.

"What a relief!" he exclaimed, as he picked his way toward us. "I heard voices and hoped you might be here."

"It is good to see you," I said. "How do you happen to be down in the valley?"

"It was just after the first rumble that I met Rolfs coming out of the forest. He told me you had passed him and I immediately got an umbrella, told the Duke I was going in search of you, and started off. I have been quite alarmed, and am more relieved than I can say."

I smiled and gave him my hand, when my saleslady remarked drily:

"Well, as three's a crowd and it ain't rainin' any more I guess I'll waltz. Pleased to meet you, Lady Helen. I kin alwus see a real flesh and blood Lady of the nobility now when I'm readin' the 'Herald' or —— —— ——'s * lovely novels. Good-bye. Hope you'll git up the mountin O. K." And she took herself and her feathers out of the ruin.

"I think we had better start for home," said Mr. Rogers. "Your brother and Lady Agatha will be so anxious."

"But you must be tired——"

"Not in the least. Do you think no one can walk but the English?" This with a smile and intonation that took all abruptness out of it.

We left the church and in a few moments were climbing the mountain, a doubly difficult task now that the logs were slippery with rain. But the forest was so green and dripping, the sun flecks glittered in the rain-drops, the depths looked so dark and wet, and full of sweet fragrant mystery! The odour of the balsam came down to us with a

* Deletion by the publisher.

rush. Mr. Rogers is a pleasant companion at all times, but I like him particularly in the forest. He seems to need it so, to be so grateful for it. I fear I have only a dim inkling of what this brief dip into the wilderness means to the tired nervous practical New Yorker.

"I hear you want to leave us," he said presently.

"Only for a few days. I am curious to see other lakes and other parts of the forest."

"And other people? I am afraid you do not like my friends as well as I had hoped."

"Ah! you are wrong," I exclaimed with the warmth of insincerity. "They interest me tremendously. They are too clever for me, that is all. I don't feel up to them."

"You are far cleverer than any of them," he replied, turning upon me that *approving* expression of which I have written, and smiling a trifle of warmth into his grave face. "Many of them are beginning to admit it quite frankly. The American nature is very generous, I assure you."

"Mrs. Laurence and Mr. Rolfs never have admitted anything of the sort, I'll wager," I cried gaily.

"Well — no; but you see they are rather spoiled."

"Nor Mr. William Lee Randolph," I said, alluding to an author who arrived two days ago. "I dreamed all last night of cutting his conceit into little bits and watching them fly together again and cohere as snugly as if nothing had happened."

"You are a severe critic, dear Lady Helen ——"

"It *is* horrid of me to criticise your friends. And after your many-sided kindness! I feel a rude little beast."

"If you were not frank with me about everything I should be greatly disappointed. And—I am quite willing to admit it to you—your frankness is very refreshing to me. I get very tired of all this posing and hero-worship and these everlasting fads. But they are inevitable in all circles where certain of its members have accomplished great things and others feel that their rôle is to admire extravagantly if they would keep their heads above water and feel in the swim."

"Do *you* think Mr. Rolfs and Mrs. Laurence and Mr. Randolph great?" I asked pointedly. "Now, you be just as frank as I am for once."

He hesitated a moment, then said: "I believe there is no admission I would not make to you, if you only gave me sufficient encouragement. Be careful of that mud hole—these stones are better. I do wish you would wear rubbers. Frankly then I do not think that any of my authors are great, but I think it best to convince the world that they are because they are unquestionably on the right track and their success will encourage the younger talent to follow in their footsteps, crowning the achievement of to-day with the richer harvest of a more virile generation. I am quite aware that we lack virility, but when a more full-blooded generation does arrive think of the vast advantage it will have in this skeleton example of flawless art and perfect taste."

"It seems to me more likely that there will be a violent reaction," I said. "That they will smash your porcelain skeleton to smithereens and build a big rude lusty giant in its place."

"Oh, I hope not," he said anxiously, "I hope not. That *would* be a life-time thrown away."

It was the first time I had heard him sigh, and the momentary unconscious appeal to my sympathy touched me sharply.

"You *have* lived for something besides self!" I exclaimed. "I believe you actually have given your best energies, and all your time and much of your fortune to building up an Art in your country that future generations may be benefited by and proud of. I do hope for your sake that it will be a success."

He turned to me with such a glow on his face that I realized I had gone too far for once, and had a wild desire to pick up my skirts and run headlong into the forest. I must say he looked handsome and most attractive. It seemed to me that I felt something glow and leap beside me, something that I never had admitted the existence of, but which gave him a distinct fascination. I could not run, and heaven knows what might have happened next. But at that moment a turn of the road brought us face to face with Mr. Nugent.

"Oh!" he exclaimed, "Oh! *What* a relief. I knew of course that Rogers would find you—but what might have happened before—Were you in the woods during the storm?"

"I was in the Catholic Church with a sales-lady from New York who demanded so much solace that I had no time to be frightened, myself." I plunged at once into a description of the adventure, out of kindness to Mr. Rogers as much as to disembarrass the situation. I knew the violent reaction within him—and I hoped he was communing with his soul in good healthy swear words.

When I did not talk, Mr. Nugent did, and Mr. Rogers' silence was well covered. Not that he did not recover himself almost immediately, and occasionally put in an apt remark.

Finally Mr. Nugent dismissed the subject of sales-ladies with his usual abruptness.

"I think I can say that I have persuaded your

brother and sister to let you go to-morrow," he said. "I demonstrated the absurdity of such slavish adherence to the conventions in this wilderness. Your maid is chaperonage enough for a few hours' trip, to say nothing of the fact that Hunter and another man will carry your trunk behind us down the mountain and that still another man with a buckboard will meet us in the valley."

My eyes danced. "What a lark!" I exclaimed. "To really go on a trip without Bertie or Agatha. But *will* they consent?"

"I am sure they will. I told them that if they insisted upon it my sister would come for you, and although of course they would not hear of such a thing I think that clinched them. So be prepared to start to-morrow morning at eight."

And, Polly, I really believe I am going! My love to you.

HELEN.

P. S. I almost apologize to Mr. Rolfs. This evening at the Club House when Mrs. Hammond was sitting forward and monopolizing the conversation, as she always does when Mrs. Laurence does not happen to be present, and delivering her entirely commonplace opinions with a vigour of enunciation and a raptness of expression which convince the unanalytical that she is quite the reverse of the little goose she is, Mr. Rolfs suddenly turned to me with such an expression of ferocious disgust that involuntarily I moved closer to him.

"*That* is what we have to write for!" he exclaimed. "There are thousands, tens of thousands of these damned fool women that we have to write down to and pose to if we want to make our bread and butter."

I almost gasped. "What on earth do you mean?" I asked.

"Oh, I like you. You've got horse sense and see through the whole blamed show. You think I'm an ass, and I am. I have to be. I nearly starved trying to be a man, so I became an emasculated backboneless poseur to please the passionless women and the timid publishers of the United States. To please the sort of American woman who makes the success of a novelist—the faddist and the gusher—you must tickle her with the idea that she is a superior being because she has no passion and that you are creating a literature which only she can appreciate—she with a refinement and a bleached and laundried set of tastes which have made her a tyrannical middle-class enthusiast for all that is unreal and petty in art!"

"Oh!" I said, "Oh!"

"I wish I had been born an Englishman," he pursued viciously. "To be great in English literature you've only to be dull; but to be great in American literature you've got to be a eunuch."

Letter VII

From the Lady HELEN POLE *to the Countess of* EDGE *and* ROSS.

Chipmunk Lake,
July 27th

Dear Polly:

MR. NUGENT, the all conquering, arranged it, Polly dear, and here I am at a far more beautiful lake than Boulder—which seems tamely pretty in comparison. It is on top of another mountain surrounded by another dense forest which grows down into the very water; but there the resemblance ends. Although not large it is almost like four different lakes, so irregular and cut up is it. From the natural terrace on which the four camps are built you look over a small body of brown water fringed with reeds and water lilies to two mountain peninsulas which jut so far into the lake as almost to close it. The opening is called The Narrows and just beyond and across the distance runs another high sloping mountain quite cutting off further view except of far pale peaks. It is only when you are in a boat beyond The Narrows that you see the lake's three other parts, one end closed up with great rocks and floating logs, but with the avenue of the inlet showing beyond; everywhere else, the dense silent forest, the spruce crowding to the front, the water lilies and their pads spreading almost to the middle of the lake. There are white lilies and yellow ones and a miniature variety with so sweet and intoxicating a fragrance that in the early morning you feel as if the boat were cutting a visible passage through it. And the mountains, mountains, everywhere.

The four cottages are made of logs, three with the bark on, the other peeled and polished. Mrs. Van Worden's is the largest and also the most homelike. We arrived rather late. Mr. N. and I, tired of the "buckboard," had left it and walked on ahead, arriving quite noiselessly. I never shall forget how comfy Mrs. Van Worden's living-room looked as we peered a moment through the glass door before knocking. It is a long low room with heavy beams across the dark red paper of the ceiling, and a red brick fireplace from floor to roof—in which great logs were blazing. In one corner was a graceful staircase, and on the "sealed" gold-coloured walls were many prints and photographs of sporting life in the Adirondacks. In one corner was a divan piled with cushions and draped with silk, a lamp swinging from the canopy. Against another wall was a straight divan, on which a young man was lying, reading a book. Then there were mounted deer heads and rugs and tables and at least eight rocking-chairs—I am going to take back a "rocker" as a present for you.

Mrs. Van Worden, who was standing with her foot on the fender staring into the fire, seemed to feel our presence in a moment, for she turned about suddenly and came swiftly to the door. And then the warmth of her welcome quite dissipated the misgivings I had felt about descending in this summary fashion upon a complete stranger. I like her better than any woman I have met in the country and as we sat up talking half the night, I already know her quite well.

She is tall and thin, with no figure exquisitely dressed—though with much more simplicity than the fashion of Boulder Lake would dictate. But these women *have* to dress so much oftener during other parts of the year that they are more disposed to a complete rest up here. Still, they can't help dressing well. Her figure's only "points" are the hands and feet, which are so small that I stare at them almost rudely. Nevertheless the hands look extremely determined. She is not pretty but has rather the beauty of individuality. Her complexion is dead white, almost transparent, and her nose irregular, but she has great glowing black eyes, a sensitive and beautiful mouth, and soft mahogany-brown hair charmingly arranged. She is about six-and-thirty, I should say, and when she hinted to me that she was nine-and-twenty I felt disposed to offer her my confidence without reserve. Never trust a woman who will not lie about her age after thirty. She is unwomanly and unhuman and there is no knowing what crimes she will commit.

The man on the divan—a long clean-limbed smooth faced delightful looking young fellow, with a humourous mouth, a frank eye and a fine high-bred *University* air about him—stood up as soon as we entered and was presented as Mr. Latimer of New York. Mr. Van Worden is a banker, very business-like and absent minded, and years older than his wife.

We had the jolliest little supper in one corner of the living room—at least four of us did, for Mr. Van Worden was on the lake, having dined—and were waited on by the lake keeper's wife, a woman of immense weight, but so light on her feet and so deft and swift in her movements that she might have been a fairy. More of her later. She interests me very much.

After supper, as it was blowing rather hard, we all sat about the blazing logs for two hours and Mrs. Van Worden and young Latimer rattled alternately. But they did not irritate me for a moment, they were so impersonal even when talking of themselves, so really clever without seeming to be in the least aware of it, so full of a humour that made no attempt at wit, and so interesting in what they had to say and in their manner of looking at things. I felt grateful enough to hug myself.

Mr. Latimer had recently been in the Philippines and he told some of his humorous adventures with a boyish abandon—I am told he is thirty but he seems much younger—that made me laugh heartily. Suddenly I caught Mr. Nugent's eye and the expression of delight on his face made me blush to my hair. We were alone for a moment just before going to bed and he whispered to me eagerly:

"You like it here! I know that you do! I am so glad."

"Oh, yes!" I exclaimed with the enthusiasm of sheer gratitude. "I do. Thank you for bringing me." Here he looked as if nothing could prevent him from kissing me and I said hurriedly:

"What a difference! It reminds me of something the Prince is rcported to have said once: 'Bright people—yes; but no damned intellect.'" Not but what I fancy the intellect is really there, Polly, but it is reserved as a substratum, from which little sparks are sent up to irradiate, not a constant conscientious blaze like an energetic thunder storm.

Mrs. Van Worden invited me into her bed-room and we muffled ourselves in warm wrappers and talked for hours while the wind howled. She really has seen the world, and is as interesting as—well, as you are. There is a woman who would sympathise with you from A to Z and never criticise. Fancy the attitude of Mrs. Laurence or Mrs. Hammond. What is Christianity, anyhow? A kind heart and a sophisticated mind?

The next morning I got up for a few moments at six and peered out of my high window. Some of the smaller trees have been cut down and I could see a little distance into the forest. It looked so quiet—so expectant. I have decided that that is the spirit of these mountain forests of the New World—expectancy, waiting. Civilisation is held in check at present by the laws of New York, which owns the greater portion of the Adirondack tract. But for how long? And they have had more than a glimpse of man, these forests, from the old dead trappers to the flowers of modern and greedy civilisation. What is it they expect? What disaster? What conquests? It seems to me sometimes as if they were holding their breath. And what are they like inside? I wish I had eyes to see? Besides the two thousand lakes there are springs, springs everywhere; there must be millions of them in the great range. From what vast subterranean flood do they burst forth? What silent potent *waiting* tides are moving unceasingly beneath the brown lakes and the riches of the forest, have been moving since the great glaciers melted?

At eight the keeper's wife, Mrs. Opp, came up with my breakfast—coffee, and "johnnie cake," and fish, fresh from the lake, and I detained her for a few moments, for she interests me unaccountably. As I said, she is very fat—she must weigh not a pound less than seventeen stone—and cannot be under five feet nine. Her face is German, but the features are small and delicately cut, and her complexion is as fine of grain as an infant's. She must be seven or eight and thirty, but her face has that virginal expression of the married woman who never has had children. Her manner is *gracious*—I cannot apply any other word to it;

but even more noticeable, I think, are her teeth and nails. They are perfect and perfectly kept. And yet she is illiterate, and has, she let fall, worked all her life. When Mrs. Van Worden is here she is both cook and housekeeper. Her husband, the keeper, is a big lithe handsome man, with regular features and a white throat. In his rough costume he looks the ideal mountaineer.

"I am not going to be lazy every day," I remarked apologetically. "But I walked nearly all the way yesterday and then sat up late."

"No wonder yor're tired," she said in her crooning indulgent voice. "A mile of it jest kills me. I git het up so, and my poor legs are *that* tired—Oh, my!" And she laughed a jolly laugh, as if, however, life were all sunshine.

"But surely you walk sometimes in these beautiful woods."

"Not very much. I git about enough walkin' round the house. When I go out of the woods in winter and visit hum fur a spell, well, then, I guess I do go about more. You see there's somethin' to go to, but up here—My! I worked in hotels mostly before I come here, so this seems kinder lonesome."

"You don't remain here in winter then? I don't blame you."

"Oh, I couldn't. It's that dismal! Frank, he comes in and out, but there ain't no real need of me stayin' here so I go home and have a real good time. I like it here. I like it here. It's as good's anywheres, only I'd have a hotel on the St. Lawrence if I could hev my choice. There'd be some life in that! Well, I must go down and not stand gassin' here. Sure you got all you want? There's lots more."

I assured her that I had more than I could possibly eat, and she smiled graciously upon me and withdrew. She is like the policeman and Jemima and the sales-lady in her unconsciousness of caste, but with a difference. What that difference is puzzles me when I have time to think about it.

July 31st

I have been here four days, Poll, and not heard the words "aristocratic" or "refined" once. Oh, blessed relief! And—yet—they just lack unselfconsciousness. Is that the word, or is it a suggestion of reserve under all their animation and candour and naturalness, a reserve that is not so much mental and personal as racial and as—well, there is no help for it—aristocratic? I think that is the explanation, after all. They *feel* themselves to be the true aristocrats of the country but are too well-bred to mention, or, perhaps, to think of it. There is just the faintest dearest little air of loftiness about them and it is so manifestly natural that I fancy it is as much the real thing as the "self-made" American. I have come to the conclusion that the modern interpretation of the Declaration of Independence is something like this: *I am as good as those that think themselves better and a long sight better than those who only think themselves as good.* When they are established on the top step like these people here, with no more flights to conquer, there is really nothing left to do but to slide down the banisters.

None of my Chipmunk Lake friends are of the "new-rich"; every fortune up here is at least three generations old, and Mr. Van W's is six. Well, they are welcome to feel themselves anything they like, for I find them wholly delightful, and they have been charming to me. Mrs. Wilbur Garrison looks rather sad and tired but is always gay in manner and interested in what other people are talking about. Mrs. Reginald Grant has several pasts in the depths of her eyes which her long lashes always seem to be sweeping aside as if it were a matter of no consequence whatever. Mrs. Meredith Jones rather goes in for charities, and Mr. Nugent says she really is a hard worker as well as a devoted mother and an irresistible coquette. She has a Greek profile, a cloud of golden hair, a Juno bust and a rather cynical mouth.

I do not know what Mrs. Hammond meant by saying there were "no men." I should say there was one apiece.

There is a young widow, a great belle, visiting Mrs. Grant—Mrs. Coward. She is very thin and not in the least beautiful, although her face lights up when she talks and has a sweet expression. But she holds herself with a calm expectancy that every man will fall at her feet, and she flatters more than any one I ever met. Then she delivers her opinions with such an air! They are usually platitudes, but you know how a manner blinds.

A Miss Page, a Southern girl, is visiting Mrs. Garrison. She has an ideal manner, is always impersonal in her conversation and seems as amiable and unselfish as possible.

The unmarried men live in the little Club House, which has a smoking-room but no dining-room. We all dine in our own camps when we are not entertaining each other, which is usually.

The children are established for the summer in other country houses, where all these people will go after their three weeks' rest from every care. The two husbands up here are quite nice, and devoted to sport. When the fish won't play in this lake they tramp off to others.

But enough of the people. I am going to tell you of the weirdest experience I ever had. Save it for me, Polly, for if ever I write a book I certainly shall put it in.

First—Last evening at sundown several of us—

two in a boat—went out on the lake in the hope of seeing the deer come down to drink. The men paddled, making so little noise and movement that the boat seemed gliding by itself through the silences of space. There was a yellow glow in the West—the aftermath of the most magnificent amber sunset; mountains and lakes of molten cloud—but the stars were not out and there was only that light from nowhere through which the vision gropes surely but always with surprise.

Mr. Nugent paddled our boat—he sat in the stern, I in the bow, with my back to him—through the Narrows, then, after drifting about for a few moments pointed toward the shore most distant. I had been warned not to speak, and not a word had been uttered when a low suppressed voice from behind gave me a start. "Look, look!" it said, "do you see? straight ahead." I saw! A reddish brown something was walking along the bank and in a moment I saw it toss its horns. But it was not of the deer I thought just then but of the strange sense of intimacy that suppressed voice on the darkening silent lake had aroused in me. In a moment it came again, lower still, for we were nearing the shore. "There is another." And he steered through the water lilies.

A mate had joined the buck and they cropped and drank for a few moments, then walked along the shore and into an arbour-like opening of the forest, exactly like people making a stately exit from the back of a stage. Almost immediately two does came bounding out of the forest and waded into the water until only their heads and red backs were visible. We remained motionless, almost breathless, but in a few moments they must have noticed us for they made hotly for the shore. When they reached it they stood for at least five minutes with their heads thrown back staring at us. Then, although we were, apparently, as lifeless as the lily pads, their reasoning faculty must have satisfied them that we were aliens and therefore to be feared, for they suddenly turned their backs and made for the forest as hard as they could go, leaping over one high bush after another, until nothing could be seen but the white lining of their tails. Then the exhibition being over we talked all the way home, and that strange sense of intimacy with a note of mystery in it was dispelled.

It was to be renewed, however, for we had not done with the deer. That night at eleven o'clock, when Mr. Van Worden was sound asleep—he really is very dull—Mrs. Van W. and I Mr. Nugent and Mr. Latimer stole down to the boat house by the light of a lantern. We were muffled up in the darkest things we possessed and I felt exactly as if we were conspirators, or smugglers, or refugees from justice.

In the boat house the men lit a lamp they had brought and placed it in a wooden case, open in front, which was on the end of a pole about three feet high. (This light is called a Jack.) The pole was set into a hole on the bow of the boat Mr. N. intended to paddle, and it was to serve as a sort of search light, not only to see the deer by, but to fascinate what moth-like instinct they possessed.

All prepared, we pushed silently out into the lake. Can you imagine the scene? The mountains—there are so many of them!—were black. The sky seemed dropping with its weight of stars. The clear glassy lake reflected the largest of them and the black masses of the forest that rose straight from its brink. And just ahead of me—shall I ever forget it?—floated a white mist, rising and falling, writhing into a different semblance every moment, the light making it the more ghostly and terrifying. I could not see a living thing; the other boat was behind us and I was in the bow as before, staring at that ghostly mist, quite forgetting the deer. A line of Tennyson's haunted me:

"The dead steered by the dumb went upward with the flood,"

and I longed to utter it aloud, but dared not. Once I turned my head to see if Mr. N. were really there. He looked black and graven, as if indeed he were the dumb servitor. The others I could not see at all. And again there was that sense of gliding, unpropelled, through the silences of the upper Universe, only a thousand times intensified. And, surely, never were so many stars gathered together before. It seemed to me that the big ones must drop into the lake, they looked so heavy, and so close, and the little ones were like a million grains of golden sand. I thought of Grimm's Fairy Tales and the princess who carried a robe of stars in a nut-shell.

But more often I watched that white mist, just in front of the prow and me, and nowhere else. Where did it come from? I have no idea. They tell me there was a mist everywhere, and that by the aid of our light we saw it just ahead, but I saw none of it elsewhere, and I saw the stars and the trees in the lake.

We must have floated for a half hour, searching almost every inch of the banks without a glimpse of deer, when Mr. N.'s paddle stopped suddenly. At the same moment I heard a slight trampling in the brush close by, then a louder, as if a great buck had been brought to bay and were pawing up the earth. Then there was a terrific snort—I had no idea anything could snort so loud—then a long warning whistle, then another snort, and another. By this time he had made up his mind to flee the danger, for the snorts were accompanied by a crashing through the brush in the opposite direction. The faster he went the louder he snorted, until distance tempered the sound. It must have been five minutes before the last faint note of his anger came back to us.

"I am afraid he has warned off all the others," came that low hoarse whisper from behind me, and it was the last touch needed to deepen the mystery of that unreal midnight.

Mr. N. paddled for ten or fifteen minutes longer, then giving it up, made for the boat house. We glided in noiselessly and he helped me out at once and extinguished the light. Then we stood on the narrow pier between the boat and the other slip of enclosed water waiting for Latimer and Mrs. Van W. There was no sign of them on the dark lake for several moments, and we were obliged to stand very close on that strip of wood in the darker boat house. I can assure you it was very weird; but with a man like Mr. N. beside one it was impossible to feel frightened. In the boat he seemed so far away. Of course I imagined that all sorts of things had happened to the others, but presently they came gliding toward us and into the boat house. We all stole home—without a word. It was long before I fell asleep.

HELEN.

Letter VIII

From the Lady HELEN POLE *to the Countess of* EDGE *and* ROSS.

Chipmunk Lake,
August 4th

Dear Polly ?

I HAVE solved the mystery of Mrs. Opp, and it has been the cause of much thought and speculation on my part. Her father was a German noble, high in favour of his Kaiser some fifty years ago. For some reason he fell from grace and was expatriated, his estates confiscated. He came to this country with a large family, drifted to one of the Northern counties of New York State and tried to make a living by farming. Of course he was a failure, poor man, but he was highly respected in the humble community, not only for his worthy character, but because he could read and write in seven languages. It was also known that he corresponded with Bismarck. Some twelve years after his arrival in the New World his youngest child was born—she who now is Mrs. Opp, wife of the keeper of Chipmunk Lake. By that time he was a common farmer and woodsman, working fourteen hours a day with his sons for a bare living, with neither the money nor the time to educate his superfluous children. The little girl grew up in the woods, turning her hand to everything, from milking to making syrup from the maple trees. When her father died and the farm was divided she "hired out," and supported herself until she married, some ten years ago.

There you have the key to the mystery; the unconscious pride of carriage, the gracious manner, the well-kept teeth and nails, the more than suggestion of breeding in her face. But all this becomes strange only when you realize her absolute unselfconsciousness. I have talked with the woman over and over again and it is as plain as her descent that she has not the slightest appreciation of what she is and has been deprived of, much less cherishes any pride or vanity in it. It is all unconscious, this persistence of inherited instincts through the most unfavourable circumstances, with not an impulse in the brain to guide it. And how short it stops, this heredity! It goes so far and no farther; the brain, most important of all, is choked with the weeds of a bitter fate. Still, she is happy—why should I pity her? She has her handsome woodsman, her placid mountain life, that eternal *youngness* in her face. Courts could give her nothing more; rather, would they give her too much.

But how it sets one to thinking, Polly. I have tried to imagine myself in similar circumstances: Dad exiled with a large brood, myself born on a mountain farm, "hired out"——The respectable amount of brain I had inherited from a long line of brilliant and useful men would be as surely mine as now—but with nothing put into it, *could* it have been wholly ignorant and unambitious and unsuspecting? *Could* I have cooked without protest for Mrs. Van Worden while her distinguished brother addressed me merely to demand more potatoes or the pepper? *Could* I have been content with finger nails and teeth, and a backbone with a pride the brain had forgotten? Oh, no! I cannot imagine it. I should have demanded schooling, read my father's correspondence with Bismarck, fed myself with his nightly tales of past splendour, and married an American of the *haute noblesse*—in short, my heredity would have worked itself out along the lines of the conventional novel, that is always so pleasantly prone to give you life as it should be, not as it is. Here I am face to face with a fact I never have met in fiction, and I am grateful for it—even while I feel sad as I speculate upon a fate I happily have escaped. The Fact is Mrs. Opp of noble blood and low degree, jolly, hearty, happy, unwarped by what she knows not of, ungrammatical—and ambitious for a hotel on the St. Lawrence river. Surely, there is a motif for a novel of advanced realism.

I have talked it over with Mr. Nugent. He is so interesting and illuminating to talk anything over with. We take long walks and rows every day. He is my constant cavalier, for it would be really unprincipled of me to attempt to cut any of these women out, they have been so sweet to me. A party of us always start off together, but there are so many paths in the forest!

I cannot analyze for you, Polly, the stage at which I have arrived with Mr. Nugent. He has not actually *said* anything, so far—he is too clever—but he has a faculty of embracing me with an invisible presentment of himself, which is very disturbing. I don't know what to think—except that I think a great deal about him. It is very sweet—but if only I could be sure. He is so different—everything over here is so different from anything I have ever known. (I don't idealize him. I wonder if that is fatal?)

5th

We do not play intellectual games here, thank heaven, and there is no idol on a pedestal, nor one person who is more the fashion than another. We are frivolous usually, although I have occasionally heard some solid and instructive conversation, and we all read a good deal. Every house has several shelves of books, and the best literature of all countries except the Great Republic is well represented. Although I no longer take much interest in the subject—and indeed had observed long ago that the Americans of this class cared little for their own bookmakers—I asked Mrs. Van Worden the other day the cause of it. She often answers in sentences so short they sound like epigrams; however, brevity is the soul as well as the substance of most epigrams, as far as I am able to distinguish between the short sentences of the witty novelists and the paragraphs of those who think. For some reason the staccato movement supplies a meaning of which the words reck not.

Mrs. Van W. shrugged her flexible little shoulders when I called her attention to the fact that she had only three American novels in her bookcase.

"Why should I waste my little time on the obvious? I read what I do not know. I want knowledge. Not of a new dialect and pin point on a map, but of life, of the eternal mysteries. I want the wisdom of those who are not afraid to live and tell of what they have felt, thought, done. I am not satiated, not blasée. I am still full of hopes and dreams, and often I am quite happy; but *I* have lived. Therefore I want to read books by people who have lived more. How could the surface—painted in water-colours by a cautious hand—interest *me*. And the love scenes! Rotten. Conducted through a telephone. I want books written out of a brain and heart and soul crowded and vital with Life, spelled with a big L. I want poetry bursting with passion. I don't care a hang for the 'verbal felicities.' They'll do for the fringe, but I want the garment to warm me first. Good God! how little true poetry there is in our time; and I often feel the want of it so terribly. I know the old boys by heart. Oh, for a new Voice! What is the matter with the men, anyway? Women make asses of themselves when they try to be passionate and rhyme at the same time, but I can see no reason why a man should become so offensively ladylike the moment he becomes a poet."

"These are busy times," I suggested. "Perhaps the virile brains have found something better to do. A poet always has seemed to me a pretty poor apology for a man. Byron was masculine but he was the great exception. And his genius of personality was far greater than his poetical gift, great, creatively, as that was. I could stand a man being a poet incidentally, if he had the power to make me forget he was a poet, but not otherwise."

And then we all went out on the lake in the dusk and Mr. Nugent quoted Byron to me for an hour. Not to my back. He was rowing this time.

6th

About two miles from here is a lake entirely covered with water-lilies. It is seldom that a boat cuts the surface or a fish line is cast, for the water is too warm for trout, and our fishermen disdain bull heads and sunfish. Consequently the green lily pads have spread over every inch of it, and scattered upon them are the waxen cups with their golden treasure. It is a scene of indescribable beauty and peace, and the low hills above the shore, instead of the usual haughty mountains, are almost as sweet and wildly still.

The keeper carried a boat there yesterday, and Mr. N. rowed me about for an hour. I gathered an armful of the lilies and hung them all over my hat and gown, linking the long soft stems in my belt until they trailed to my knees. I felt so happy in catching at the beautiful things as the boat grinded through their hidden part, and in adorning myself, that I quite forgot Mr. N., who had fallen silent. The silence of one of these Americans, by the way, is quite different from that of our men. They are at so much pains usually to entertain and interest a woman that their silences indicate either a pleasant intimacy, or depression, never a lordly superiority to small matters. Therefore, I suddenly paused with a cluster of lilies half raised and directed my glance to my companion. He looked neither musing nor sad. His eyes were fastened upon me with eager admiration, his whole face, that lean powerful nervous face stamped by unconquerable emotions, was so concentrated, that I felt myself blushing vividly, and I waved the cluster of lilies at arm's-length.

"Did you ever see anything so beautiful?" I exclaimed gaily. "Is there any flower in the world so artistic as the water-lily?—from its pure cold form to its aloofness from the leaves?—and always alone, never a blossom and its buds, never a group, gathered as if in fragrant gossip. It is the nun among flowers, sexless, childless, angelically pure and cold, asking nothing of this life but to bloom white and unspotted in some mountain convent like this, a convent of perpetual silence, with its wall of hills, its roof of blue, embroidered with gold at night and haunted by day with fleecy clouds that look like wandering angels—Oh, dear! I forgot the thunderstorms and the cries of angry deer, but doubtless the lilies merely close up at such unholy sounds and pray in unruffled serenity."

"Lady Helen, will you marry me?" asked Nugent.

Polly, I gave such a start that the boat rocked, and I felt like a silly girl who never had been proposed to before. Moreover, I blushed scarlet. But, although I had, over and over, imagined his proposal, none of my conceptions had been anything like this. I had pictured him losing his head suddenly when we were walking alone in the woods, or keeping guard over the fire in the living-room at night. I had—well, there is no use going into details of what did not happen. Suffice it to say that the proposal was delivered in tersest English under a four o'clock sun, while he had an oar in each hand. And as I could not run away, and as he gave me not the slightest excuse to be angry there was nothing to do but to give him some sort of reply.

"To be perfectly honest, I don't know," I said.

"You mean that you are not sure that you love me, but that I may hope," and his face turned as crimson as mine—no easy feat, for it is about the colour and consistency of leather.

"It is the sort of thing you can put in a good many different ways. And there is so much to be considered. You have the double magnetism of mind and sex, you always interest and never bore me, and you are entirely different from any one I have ever known. I am twenty-six, and like all women, eager to be in love—that I never have been makes my longing for that particular heritage the keener. Moreover, I am on the rebound from two years of cruel anxiety, days and nights of tears and waiting. For the first time I feel that I belong to myself once more, that the world and all its delights are mine—and you happen to be the only man. How it would be if I had met you in England in every-day conditions—that is the problem I cannot solve. These wild mountains, this life full of novelty, the novelty of everything—Oh, I don't know."

"Have you any prejudice against marrying an American?"

"No prejudice. That is not the word. It is—well, the very novelty that draws me to you is what I am most afraid of. You see—as I said—I never met any one in the least like you before. The men I have known, whether Englishmen or Europeans, are all men born of the same traditions as myself. Fundamentally they are the same, no matter what their individualities. But you—you are just as different fundamentally as every other way. How do I know but that your great attraction for me is partly the spell of your fascination, more still the novelty which appeals to my somewhat various mind?"

"You certainly have given the matter some thought," he said, smiling with a sort of joyous sarcasm, but in his usual harsh abrupt tones. "I'll debate the matter if you like. Your uncertainty of mind is due to the fact that you have gone fancy free to the age of twenty-six. Unless a woman early acquires the habit of falling in love, it becomes more difficult every year—the disassociating of the mind from the emotions—the surrender of self—you struck me when I first saw you as being so implacably proud in your absolute self-ownership—it was delicious—I knew you never had kissed any man—when will you give me your answer?"

"When? Oh! Well—before—" brightening—"when Bertie is quite well."

"Your brother is as good as well now. Soulé says there isn't a microbe in him. The Adirondacks and common sense are all he wants. He has acquired both. Can you assert that you know it would be utterly impossible to love me?"

"Oh, no, I can't say that."

"Then take the plunge. I will answer for the rest. You won't love me before you marry me. I feel sure of that. I am equally sure that you will love me after. And all the differences from your traditional man—they will transpose themselves into commonplaces when they have become the familiar details of daily life."

"But Englishwomen never marry American men," I exclaimed, grasping wildly at a straw. "It always is the other way."

"There lies your chance for fame," he said more lightly than one would expect from his face. "You are already the most delightfully original of women. Don't do anything so commonplace as to go home, after having all your blood made over by the Adirondack air, and marry a great landlord with a rent-roll and six titles. Fancy the stimulation of watching a determined American throttling a fortune out of his chaotic country, helping him in his ambitious career, rising with him step by step until he is head and shoulders above the seventy struggling millions of the United States of America. Does not the prospect please you? You see I am practical. I hate self-control. I know very little about it. But I dare not be lover-like, not the least bit, till you give me permission."

"Oh, please don't! Yes, the life *would* be interesting. But I adore politics. Would you throw over that Trust and go in heart and soul for reform, with the ultimate intention of being a distinguished statesman?"

"Yes—but it would mean a curtailed income."

"I have quantities of money—it *would* be rather an original international match, wouldn't it?"

"It certainly would. And while you could expend your entire income on dress and jewels if you chose, you would have to make up your mind to live according to *my* income."

"Oh!"

"I *should* be a failure if I settled down to live on a woman's money at my age—forty-one—; moreover my divorce from the interests of capitalism would be deprived of its point. It would be the sacrifice that would tell most in the beginning. No native of the British Isles would be accused of the disinterestedness of marrying an unwealthy American when protected by a rent-roll. Nobody would suspect your income."

"That is a nice polite thing to say to me! How would you like the idea of people saying I married you to be supported—with the inference that no one in England would have me?"

"I do not care a red cent what any one says or thinks if I get you. That is the only thing in life that interests me at present."

"Bertie might oppose it so violently that he would have another hemorrhage."

"If he were convinced that you loved me and if you wept a few judicious tears, common gratitude would force him to consent without a hemorrhage—and if you postponed the announcement a month he couldn't have another if he tried. Besides, he loves you devotedly—you know his opposition would soon be exhausted. I have seldom seen a brother and sister so united. He would end by feeling with you and making vivid mental pictures of your great desire for happiness—if I could only create that desire in you."

"Oh, dear!" I said. "You must give me time. I *can't* say anything definite for days and days. *Please* talk of something else."

"I have no intention of worrying you. Let us land here. I have another lake to show you. If this is a cloister, rapt and holy, that is a refuge for lost souls, dank and sinister."

Much interested, and delighted at his ready conformity to my wishes, I stepped ashore and followed him along a "runway" (deer run), for about a mile. It turned and twisted through the wood and sometimes we had to climb over fallen trees, not having the lightsome feet of the deer—who could leap a house, I should think. It was not a dense wood, and the sunlight fairly tumbled in, but so divided that it seemed palpable enough to catch by the apronful. Some of the leaves looked to be made of light, and a sea-gull—they nest in these forests—seemed swimming and drinking in an upper lake of sunshine. But, abruptly, this charming impression was behind us. The wood grew dark and I noticed that the ground was very springy and soft—as our moors are in places.

"We are on a swamp—made of the decay of trees for a hundred years—" he said—"but you are quite safe. It is at least five feet deep."

This was sufficiently creepy—only five feet of rotted bark and leaves between ourselves and the lake—although I reflected that if it could support trees, our additional weight would not sink it—but in a moment we stood on the brink of the lake.

Polly, I never have seen so desolate a spot. Even the mountains had deserted it. The forest about it grew on land as flat as a plain, and the trees hid the peaks which were only a few miles distant. And so many of the trees were dead. Lightning had blasted them and scarcely a spruce had escaped the blight. All about the shore the lake was choked with rotting trunks, their naked branches projecting starkly above the water—which had no movement. Its tarnished surface, as ripless as a marsh, did not even reflect that deserted wood—they held themselves aloof from each other; and yet they seemed dying together. The lake has no inlet, Mr. N. had told me as we came along; it is fed by springs and the moisture of the forest. I could imagine it dropping lower and lower, as the trees about it died, until—a century hence?—a dry bed choked with rotting trees would be visited as the tomb of one of Nature's failures. In England such a spot would be the headquarters of a dozen dark and terrible stories, and would have done threadbare duty in fiction. But old as it is it is still too young for that complicated thing called life to have centred about it. It is on one of the New World's peaks, and not in another generation will she have time to discover it. It is like those unhappy mortals who die and rot before they have guessed that there is aught in the world to live for. Poor stranded ugly duckling. I felt more pity for it than terror and almost resented the calm insolence of its beautiful fellows—two thousand of them, I am told. I wondered if its hidden springs met and gossipped with other springs, who in turn poured their cold freshness into other lakes, and with it their tale of a comrade forgotten by Nature and despised by man. Doubtless they would deepen their amber-brown in scorn, those spoilt beauties of the mountains, worshipped of men and darlings of Nature; not a ripple of pity would agitate them, I would vow.

"Look," said Mr. N.

He pushed his feet hard against the swamp, putting much spring into his body—and for a hundred yards the shore trembled, the trees moved as if on a seesaw. My nerves are strong, but that was too much. I grasped his arm.

"Come!" I said, "Take me away—please. And do you go ahead. I want to look at a living being till I get out of this wood."

And we went back to the lake of the water-lilies, that looked pure, and sweet, and happy enough to pray for their lost neighbour.

7th

This morning I sat watching the sunlight play on the wrinkles of the lake where a light breeze blew. The glittering sun-flecks looked exactly like a flock of tiny silver birds caught fast on the surface of the lake and straining their wings even to run away. Everyday I find something new in this lake to interest me, and early this morning, being unable to sleep, I rose and looked out of my front window and saw a great deer, with his antlers against the rosy dawn, standing on one of the points of The Narrows. For a few moments he listened intently, then waded out among the lily pads and had his morning repast.

Perhaps you can imagine why I slept so ill last night. Polly, I wish I knew my own mind. I am afraid of making a mistake and afraid of throwing away what may be my one supreme opportunity to love. If I were only an American or he an Englishman. If only I had the intuitive knowledge of him and all that he will mean. I am beginning to suspect that I have something of the pioneer, of the discoverer in me. After all, why should not one make great experiments in life? Obedience to traditions, to habit, we see every day—and how much happiness?

But I think I'll be glad to get away from the subject for a time.

I am rather keen for the autumn to come—"the fall of the year"—when all these mountains are a blaze of red and gold and the lakes reflect their glory; when the dew freezes on these forest flames and turns them to jewels that outdazzle the stars; when the hunters with their red caps are in them, not stalking the nimble deer, but sitting beside the runways hour after hour, patiently waiting the passing of the only lords left in these forests, when we have venison three times a day and wonder why we pined for it. There! that was as malicious a drop as any of Heine's, and I am sorry.

I saw such a laughable sight two days ago. Mr. N. took me to the cow-yard to see it. Know first that the deer flies are a pest in the land and the terror of beasts. The solitary cow the colony boasts was taking her afternoon nap, down on her folded legs. Close to her head and perched along her back were a half dozen hens with their heads alert, watching the circling flies. The moment one lit, the nearest chicken pounced and the fly disappeared, never to torment cow or deer again. I saw ten disposed of in this way, while the cow slumbered peacefully, secure in her guard.

Have I told you that there is a deep ravine on one side of the house? The veranda overhangs it and I often stand and stare down into that wild tangle of fallen trees and rocks and ferns. The sides are broken and steep and under the shade of many trees, straggling up into complete darkness. The torrent is almost dry, but in winter and spring it is broad and noisy and all the ferns are covered and show green and lace-like under the water. It is the outlet of the lake and it goes far down into the valley where it tumbles over a fall into another and wider stream. Up this rocky steep mountain brook, over the cascade, the trout climb in their thirst for the cold springs of the higher lakes. No other fish can make that perilous journey, so Chipmunk is one of the stars of the Adirondacks. The trout have no minnows or other small fish to feed on, and rise to the fly with little coaxing. I am become so learned in mountain lore! But I feel as if I had discovered this wonderful country, and as happy as a poet in the nervous languor of creation.

You remember I wrote you of Mrs. Coward—and, by the way she says she met you at Homburg and in Scotland two years ago—I have concluded that I do not like her quite as well as the others, not because she is insatiable in her desire for admiration and has several times flattered Mr. N. right out of the room and on to the lake—how can men be so weak?—when he is palpably devoted to me and therefore in common decency she should let him alone. Unless she mends her ways I shall turn my batteries on Mr. Carlisle, a dashing young millionaire who distinguished himself in the late war, is a master of hounds, drives a Tally-ho, is a champion at golf, never misses the two deer a season the government permits him to shoot, and is altogether very jolly and charming. I could cut her out if I chose and without flattering the animal either. That is a trick of the mind to cover up the defects of nature.

But what I started to say was that the real reason I dislike her is that I have discovered more of the snob in her than in most of these Americans, aspiring as they are—with the possible exception of Mrs. Laurence. Yesterday morning I "dropped" into Mrs. Grant's lodge, and while the servant went for Mrs. Coward—Mrs. Grant had a headache—I picked up a framed photograph of a very good-looking young man in the uniform of the United States. I still held it when Mrs. Coward came stepping down the stairs like the duchess in the play, a red poppy in her dark hair, a soft cream-white morning gown clinging to herself and the floor—the morning was chilly. She had a bunch of poppies in her belt and altogether looked rather well.

"Is this your brother?" I asked. "I fancy I see a resemblance."

"Yes," she replied, "it is my soldier-brother. He made a brilliant charge at Santiago and I am very proud of him. Sit there, dear Lady Helen, where the light falls full on you. You are so radiant, bathed in sunlight—and you can stand it. I always feel in the presence of poetry—a blue and gold edition of all the poets—when I can sit and look at you like this. Poetry is really elevating, don't you think so?—I always maintain that, positively. It is like pure air and the rural beauties of the country. But about my brave brother: it is only fondness that makes me proud of him, for there never has been a generation in our family where we have not given at least one soldier to the country. Of course you will appreciate that. Very few American families can say that for *seven generations* its men have distinguished themselves in the field and added to the honour of the name."

Her low silken shallow voice paused that I might comment, but I only stared at the portrait—now restored to the table—trying in vain to frame a phrase that would express my awe of the seven generations. Finally, I said desperately:

"He looks—really—as if the entire Spanish army could not terrify him."

This extravagance served the purpose of diversion. "Nothing could terrify him," she exclaimed. "He only needs another war to become really famous. I am quite positive our unfortunate acquisitions will let us in for another war before long—the Chinese question—don't you think so? I think it so delightful that American women are now beginning to take as much interest in politics as English women do. You really have been our superiors in that—as in many other—respects. I heard you discussing the great questions of the day with Mr. Nugent and Mr. Carlisle last night and I quite envied you—I am just beginning, and you seem to have learned politics with your alphabet. I am *so* glad you have such influence with Mr. Nugent, because I am convinced that he has the making of a statesman in him and that it is his duty to go into high politics. I have always maintained," she added weightily, "that it is a man's duty to cultivate his gifts. If he feels an irresistible impulse to write he should do so—or to paint—or to model. Politics are of equal importance to the development of civilisation—the right sort. Do not you agree with me, Lady Helen?"

"I have always maintained that white is white, and that the sun gives light when there are not too many clouds," I said, firmly. "How wonderfully becoming those poppies are to you. I envy any one who can wear red, it is a colour so full of life, but it does not suit me at all."

For a second she had looked puzzled, but she is too thorough a woman of the world to hang out her emotions, and she replied with her usual suavity:

"If I could wear pink and dead white, and brilliant blues as you can I should resign red without a struggle. I have *never* seen anything so beautiful as you are with a pink rose in your hair and another at your throat."

But I had had as much of this as I could stand and I asked her abruptly if she had visited many of the lakes.

"This is my first visit to the Adirondacks, I am ashamed to say. I was taken abroad every summer when I was a girl and I have gone almost every year since from force of habit and because I really have such a delicious time. It is one's duty to see all the beauties of the old world, don't you think so, Lady Helen?"

But I did not want to talk about Europe. "I hear that Spruce Lake is so beautiful," I said. "Could not we—a party of us—walk over there some day? It is only seven miles, and Mr. Nugent says the trail is very good."

"Seven miles! *Dear* Lady Helen. Twice seven are fourteen. Remember—we—alas!—are not English."

"They might put us up for the night——"

"Oh, quite impossible. We do not know any of them. They are business people from Buffalo and Utica and all those provincial towns."

"In trade, do you mean?"

"That is the way you would express it. It is the same class—people who keep stores or make things."

"And they have the same tastes as yourself?" I asked, puzzled at this new American facer. "They are—sportsmen? They lead the same life up here as you do?"

"I really don't know anything about them. I suppose there are certain national characteristics; several lakes in the Adirondacks are owned by people of that sort. I am told that there was an encampment of commercial travellers just off the borders of this property last year."

"But I don't understand. Your lines of caste are very marked, it has seemed to me. Why should the leisure class and the commercial traveller have the same tastes. It is very odd."

But she refused to take the slightest interest in the subject, and that afternoon as I was walking to the lake of the water-lilies with Mr. N. I asked him for enlightenment.

"Oh, Eastern men are keen sportsmen," he said. "That is to say, most—wherever there are mountains and woods and lakes. It is an instinct inherited from the old hunters and trappers—from the days when the settlers shot game for food and were as familiar with the wilderness as the farm. These settlers were the ancestors of men who are in all classes of life to-day. And you must remember that there is no 'Continent' to run over to for the yearly vacation. You can travel an immense distance here and pay a good deal of money only to hear a change of accent. But the forests of

New York and Maine mean rest, reinvigoration, and the complete happiness of the sportsman. These men up here go in the woods every year as naturally as they keep their nose to the grindstone for the remaining ten or eleven months.

"And they are first-class sportsmen."

"As good as any in England."

"Men that—that—sell hats?"

"Carlisle is neither keener nor better."

"Certainly your country is wonderfully interesting and sometimes I feel as if I were groping about in the neighbourhood of the true democracy. Do they also play golf?"

"They do, indeed."

"The tradesmen? People who keep retail shops."

"In the small interior towns many of them have achieved sufficient prosperity and leisure, and they are very keen about it. But in the large towns it is usually the wealthier class that goes in for it; the families of business and professional men, successful on a large scale."

And then I saw the lilies.

I must tell you that Mrs. Van Worden often goes into the kitchen and sits in a rocking chair by the window and talks to Mrs. Opp, and that sometimes, when the men are out, she invites her into the living-room. It appears that unless these people were treated with a certain amount of consideration they would not remain. A city servant is a servant, but in the country they appear to have studied the Declaration of Independence, and doubtless they all know that Abraham Lincoln's sister "lived out." Mrs. Opp is quite insensible of her noble blood but she is as proud as Lucifer all the same, and because her untainted Americanism teaches her that she is "as good as anybody." She is willing to work for hire and envies no one, but the slightest display of "airs," an unthinking snub, and she would pack her bundle and march over the mountain with a majesty the self-conscious American of high degree never will achieve. It is truly delightful and I love her. I often go out and sit in the rocker and watch her great bulk move lightly about the exquisite kitchen, and listen to her kindly drawl emphasised by little gracious bends of the head. She tells me the gossip of the mountains, and alluded the other day to the cook at Boulder Lake as "a lovely woman." I told her about Jemima, and she said:

"Poor child. I guess she was right, but she didn't know how to take it. Of course you folks nat'rally wants ter eat with yourselves, and the hired help as is used to farms and little country towns don't just see how it is at first. Different people has different ways and all we ask up here is to be treated right, we don't expect the hull earth. I've always knowed that, because I've lived so much to hotels, but Jemima, I guess she's pretty green yet."

When I told her about Jemima wanting to see "a dook," she laughed heartily.

"Well, I guess I'd like to see one, myself," she admitted, "not that I'd expect them to be so different from other folks, but just because I've read so much about 'em. That's it. That's it. I'm glad he's gittin' on so nice. He had orter drink plenty of milk."

Curiously enough, that evening I received a letter from Bertie saying that another "eminent doctor" had put him on a milk diet and promised him complete health in *one* year if he would be faithful to it and the Adirondacks for that period.

"Its beastly uninteresting diet, Nell, and required all the will I've got to make up my mind to it," he wrote; "but I want to get back to England and be alive once more, so I've plunged in —literally enough. I've leased an Inn on one of the big public lakes from October till June, so we'll have a big old-fashioned house, they tell me, and not a care, for the proprietor will "run it." Rogers has promised to come up twice a month and I have written to Nugent and asked him to come often and bring all the friends he likes. I fancy from your letters that I should like the men —and women—over there better than these—Rogers excepted. I believe he is in love with you, Nell, and so is Nugent; but you mustn't marry an American. By the way Roddy Spencer is coming over here—wrote me to expect him any day, and that he'd look me up at once. He has just succeeded—old Landsburghe died last month, and left Roddy all his personal property. That must amount to three or four hundred thousand and with the estates will set up Roddy as well as he could wish—and his debts must have been a pretty penny."

I shall be rather glad to see Roddy. He was always with Bertie when they were boys, but I have not seen much of him of late years. Didn't he go to South Africa in the hope that Rhodes would put him in the way of making a fortune—after he had loaded himself too heavily with debts to remain in London. I forget the details. The legacy must have been a pleasant surprise, for the old Marquis was very eccentric and had refused to pay his debts. Well, I shall be glad to see him and suppose he is as good looking as ever.

HELEN.

Letter IX

From the Lady HELEN POLE *to the Countess of* EDGE *and* ROSS.

Chipmunk Lake,
August 11th

Dearest Polly:

I AM rather put out, and have been so irritable for two days that I hardly know myself. Still, thank heaven, nobody suspects it. I never have been more amiable.

The other night a half dozen of the party were playing Bridge in a corner of Mrs. Van Worden's living-room. I detest gambling and was trying to interest myself in a book when I happened to glance out of the window and saw—Mrs. Coward and Mr. N. on their way down to the lake. Now, I don't pretend to be in love with the man, Polly, but I do feel that while he is pretending devotion to me it is little short of an insult for him to sneak off with another woman—and an arrant coquette—for a row at nine o'clock at night—it is scandalous and I never have heard *any one* utter so many virtuous platitudes as Mrs. C. If I thought he was trying to make me jealous I should merely dismiss him from my mind with the contempt he would deserve, but he really is incapable of such pettiness, and I happen to know he was only too frightened I'd find it out.

Polly, I cannot pretend to describe to you my sensations when I saw those dark shapes steal through the spruce grove before the house—the branches are cut so high that it is really a grove of slender trunks and you see the lake plainly. For the moment I felt as if my heart were sinking and I involuntarily pushed my hand underneath it, while my breath shortened and my face burned and then went cold. I had an impulse to rush out and see if it really were true and to prevent it. And then I fell into a rage. How I wished Roddy Spencer were here. He is such a splendid looking creature that he could be made to set another man wild with jealousy. Suddenly I bethought myself of Carlisle. He was playing, but the game was nearly over. I made up my mind in an instant; I got up and moved about the room as if I were getting bored and impatient, and in a few moments I caught his eye. I sent him a glance of coquettish appeal, and it had the desired effect. The moment the game was over he was at my side and we ensconced ourselves on the three-cornered divan under the swinging rose-coloured lamp and never moved till twelve o'clock. N. and Mrs. C. returned, looking half-frozen and too silly, for they were obliged to get almost inside the chimney. We never noticed them. I coquetted, Polly, as I never coquetted before, and Mr. Carlisle is a flirt whose accomplished depths it is interesting to explore. For fear he should think I was animated by pique—although he knew nothing of the row—I contrived to intimate that I was rather bored and on the verge of making an excuse to return to Boulder Lake. At the same time I made him feel what a triumph he would achieve if he renewed the fascinations of Chipmunk Lake for me. Nothing would induce me to leave. I shall stay and prove to this self-satisfied American flirt that I can make myself twice as interesting as herself. I'll employ her own weapon, flattery, and make her platitudes apparent. When I have sufficiently punished N. I'll take him back and keep Carlisle besides. I am sure she wants to marry N. She has too large a fortune of her own to be tempted by Carlisle's, and N.'s possibilities appeal to her inordinate ambition and vanity.

This morning, of course, N. tried to be as devoted as usual. But I dismissed him with an absent smile, which became brilliantly personal the moment C. appeared. We went off for a walk in the forest and I never shall forget the expression of N.'s face. I almost relented. But he deserves punishment. I will have all or nóthing. In the afternoon Mrs. Coward drifted about majestically for a half hour or so—her face expressing nothing—while Carlisle and I read a novel together on the divan in the corner. She tried to get N. into her pocket but he merely glowered into the fire and took no notice of her. Presently she drifted away, and in the afternoon I saw her fishing with *Mr. Van Worden!* If I were in such desperate straits I would give out that I was writing a book, and keep to my room. I fancy she wove a net of flattery for Mr. Latimer, but he is a faithful soul. Mrs. Van W. often looks sad, by the way, brilliant as her normal spirits are. It must be an unsatisfactory roundabout way of trying to be happy. I am more than ever determined to make no mistake when I do marry, and to consider one thing only. I am convinced there is no other happiness.

13th

I have restored N. to favour but now give him only half my time, that he never may be quite sure of me again. Mr. C. apparently is quite as high in my good graces, and while he is merely stimulated and on the verge of becoming serious, N. shows a curious mixture of alarm, anger and energetic determination—and has taken no more rows or walks with Mrs. C. I have managed to convey to him that I will accept no divided homage, and he is now only too eager to give me the whole of it, and keeps out of Mrs. C.'s way. I must say she is a thoroughbred. She has never betrayed jealousy or pique by the flutter of an eyelash. Perhaps I'll restore Mr. Carlisle to her presently, for I am rather tired of him. There is none of the quality of the unexpected about him. He is a well-proportioned mass of good points and good fortune—all trained outward; he never has had the necessity—I believe his family has had wealth and position for four generations—nor the inclination to look very far into himself, consequently the crust has deepened and the personality diminished. Mr. N., on the other hand, while as well-born, has had all his faculties sharpened by a struggle with the impinging forces that array themselves against the young man seeking to conquer them without money. But first of all he received a college education and distinguished himself by his talents and hard study. Given the illuminating education first and the struggle of the wits for mastery afterward, and adding to both the advantages and the principles of a gentleman —and the inner life, the soul, of such a clever man could not fail to be developed, complex and interesting. I have had only glimpses of it, but it has excited my curiosity so that I naturally could not watch another woman carry him off with equanimity. But I don't think there is any danger of another lapse. He has renewed his efforts to interest me, and—it certainly *is* clever of him—has not so much as addressed me with his eyes again. That is to say there is no appeal in them. But there are other things, Polly, and there is something about the man that fearfully suggests the impossibility of failure. But the weather is so heavenly just now that I wish everybody in the world could have everything he wanted. It is like living in a crystal dome and being bathed by invisible waves of soft stimulating perfumed air; with splendid masses of rich and tender greens, of amber-browns and turquoise blue, and the golden glory of sunsets for the eye, and a vast uplifting silence. It is a sort of voluptuous heaven, virtuously seductive.

The other day several of us walked down the mountain to one of the farms to see the haying. It was a grand valley among the mountain tops. From the farm we visited we looked over rolling wooded hills, dotted with houses, cattle, and a solitary white church spire, to a great irregular chain of green mountains, encircling the horizon; other peaks, faint and blue and distant, showing beyond their depressions; and the forest, the forest, everywhere beyond the clearings of the farmers.

The hay had been cut and the mechanical rake was gathering it into heaps when we arrived, while men pitched it into a wagon where another man stood with a pitchfork pressing it down. The sweetness of that air! I never shall forget it; I was doubly glad I never had used perfumes. It was drenched with the sweetness of newly mown hay and it almost intoxicated me. I fancy that if Mr. N. had seized the occasion to press his suit—however, I do not know. He did not, and as there were some ten people in the field it would not have been so romantic, in spite of the fragrance. They gave me a hand-rake and I raked quite a good deal of the pretty green stuff that it seems shocking the farm-yard cattle should eat.

I was very much disappointed in the appearance of these mountain farmers. How few things in life resemble the traditions of them—we have been so victimized by poets and romanticists. I expected great brawny muscular fellows, with enormous legs, brown skins, and deep chests. But they are pale and thin and stooping, not one looks as if he would see sixty or as if he got the least pleasure out of life. Mr. N. explained that hard work while they were young and no cessation of it thereafter had broken their constitutions. In winter they work on the roads which they are under contract to keep open, and of course it snows and freezes heavily and frequently. During these same severe months they also go in the woods and help to "draw" the logs the lumbermen have cut during the summer for the pulp mills. These logs have to be piled on sleds and drawn to the creek, to be floated down to the valley after the spring rains. The men rise at three in the morning, working by torches till sunrise, and seldom get to bed before eleven at night! No wonder they are old men at forty. And I don't pretend to say how many cords of wood they cut a year, or how many stone fences they have built, or how many thousand stones they dug from the ground before they could farm.

When all the hay had been removed the field looked like a great green lawn—brilliantly green under the five o'clock sun. Beyond was a dip, then the thick masses of the dark green woods, touched into richer green by that blaze of sunshine, then the mountains, sombre and faintly blue. It is a beautiful land, Polly, but it depresses me to think that while it means new blood and new life and all cure for the outsider of leisure, it sucks jealously back into its own store of vitality the little store of its struggling children. It is an unnatural and snobbish mother, after all.

Mr. N. calls me "Maud Muller," since I raked the hay. Did you ever come across that Quaker poet, Whittier? He lived here in America, but I am told he is the poet of the English quakers as well. Mr. N. recited "Maud Muller" to me, as we stood apart in the field—after I had tired of raking. It really is a beautiful and musical poem, but I could not see anything quakerish about it.

When I write "I am told," Polly, you may assume that my authority is Mr. N. As far as my limited comprehension can perceive he knows everything.

16th

Mr. Carlisle was called suddenly to Newport last night by the illness of his mother. A man rode thirty miles with the telegram, left his horse at a farm house and walked the trail—which is so full of rocks logs and mud-holes that no strange horse could cover it without breaking a leg, and, likely as not, his neck. It was just after dinner and we were all grouped in the little spruce grove before the camps watching the sunset, when the man, looking so hot and tired, came hurrying out of the woods. I am sure every one of us had a fright when we saw the yellow envelope, a telegram is such a rare interloper in the peace of these mountain camps; and when the man said "Mr. Carlisle," I am equally sure that every one of us wanted to hold Mr. C.'s hand. He went rather pale, but said it was doubtless a false alarm as his mother had been very nervous ever since the war—during which her nerves had been on the rack between apprehension of Cervera's fleet and his own demise—and hastened away to get his things together. The keeper was sent out to bring a buckboard in and Mr. C. left at three this morning.

I am sorry to say, Polly, that before he left I had rather a painful interview with him. I tried to avoid it, but these American men are very determined, my dear, and he managed to detain me on the veranda after the others had gone in. How I hate men to be serious! It hurts my conscience so that I don't get over it for weeks. I had not the slightest intention of making him love me, I only wanted to punish that woman for her contemptible conduct in regard to Mr. N. Now I feel quite as bad myself and wish that I had simply contented myself with showing her that I had a string tied to Mr. N. Mr. C. is really a fine manly fellow and I felt like petting him as I would Bertie and telling him not to mind, but of course I couldn't. He vows he'll come back the moment he is free, and gently insinuated contempt for a suitor who was ten years too old to win me. How funny these men are! What I am to do with them all I am sure I cannot imagine, but I would rather he went away hoping, and accepted his fate by degrees; for heaven knows I do not wish to add too heavily to his troubles. Not that I gave him any encouragement. Heaven forbid. But they are so determined, these Americans.

The buckboard awoke me at three o'clock, and I got up and peered out of my high window. The woods looked so grey and ghostly, filled with mist that was like a wet cobweb. The keeper was driving and Mr. C. sat on the back seat muffled in a winter great coat. Mr. Latimer went out with him to the end of the trail; and presently they disappeared into the forest and the mist; and the silence was as if the world were dead.

But I have not told you of the new arrival. She has come to spend the last of our camping days here with Mrs. Wilbur Garrison, and she is quite the most imposing, nay, overwhelming person I have met in this extraordinary jumble of democracy and caste, known—infelicitously, I gather—as the United States. She is Mrs. Earle wife of —— —— —— ——,* and of course, a personage of vast importance in Washington. But

* Deletion by the publisher.

she is no mushroom; she has belonged for heaven knows how many generations—eight, perhaps—to the haute noblesse of the country and was born into an equally imposing number of dollars. But, Oh, Polly! she is so cold, so haughty, so frozen! Her handsome little head is set so far back on her mountainous body, her back bone is so rigid and her upper lip so proudly curled, there is such a touch of icy peremptoriness in her manner, as if it were her daily task to dismiss pushing aspirants for social recognition—that I feel I have looked upon the walking embodiment of the aristocratic idea as it is interpreted by Americans. Heaven knows she has been sweet to me, she has even invited me to spend a month with her in Washington next winter; but I know that after a consecutive month of that chill presence I should return to Bertie a sort of hysterical iceberg, my marrow frozen and my humour on the verge of insanity. And, although not in the least clever, she would be quite an agreeable woman were it not for her tragic self-consciousness, for she must know the world of Washington like a book; and it is a book I should like to read. But she will not talk. All she has said of Washington is to intimate her scorn of all "new-comers," her boundless *ennui* of the duties of her official position, her sacrifice of her own inherited desire for segregation from the common herd to the interests of her distinguished husband. And yet she is not ill-natured. She is as placid as Chipmunk Lake, and, I am told, an exemplary wife and mother, if *not* a radiant and fascinating hostess. Her only fault is—well—her aristocracy! I tried to interest her in the vivid people of Boulder Lake, in the farmers of the valley, in Jemima, in the various strange beings I have met in this strange country. All by way of experiment, and in vain. Her mind could not respond to the fact of their existence. They had not been born in her original circle nor thrust upon her by the exigencies of public life. She betrayed a flicker of interest in Mrs. Opp and remarked vaguely that she should have imagined blood would count for more than that, then curled her lip and relapsed into silence. Polly, what are *we?* I am oppressed sometimes with the suspicion that those countries which are not the United States are like diseases in the creed of the Christian Scientists—they do not exist. We merely imagine we are, they know we are not, but tolerate our whim. We have lost caste because we have lost our consciousness of birth, and are therefore degenerate. Upon my word, Polly, I begin to think that the snobs who run after us in England are the truest Republicans, after all. However, I have nothing to say against my other friends of Chipmunk Lake—always excepting Mrs. Coward—for they are wholly charming, and unaffected, and not afraid to let you see they know the world. Miss Page does not, and thinks well of all the world—happy, happy girl.

There is another point on which these people greatly differ from those of Boulder Lake—that is a certain homogeneity. Men and women, they are like one large family and evidently have been brought up together; and Mrs. Van Worden says that with most of her set it is quite the same. They all call each other by their first names, and there is that same utter absence of formality as with us when we are quite among ourselves. In the set at Boulder Lake there is a formality that never relaxes, they all seem to have an abnormal respect for each other, and I vow I never heard the first name of one of them. They have accumulated each and all with care, but their set is stamped with the heterogeneity of a new incident in civilisation. And they have a bourgeois timidity about expressing their real opinion—if they have any—against the ruling opinion—or fad. Each thinks as the other thinks—how often I have disconcerted them!

Mrs. Coward, by the way, preserves her unruffled demeanour and has never so much as put out a little claw and scratched me. A woman of twenty-seven with that amount of self-control should be capable of great things. She never has overdone it, never for a moment. (I wonder if she has anything up her sleeve.)

I did not tell you, she informed me the other day that she is a "Colonial Dame," and *has her family tree*—with two Presidents and ten statesmen on collateral twigs—*framed and hung in her library at New-*

port. Polly, what *do* you make of that. I ventured to speak to Mrs. Van Worden about it, and she said:

"Rot. Fads. We all think that the Almighty made Heaven first and the United States just after—pickling it till Europe and Asia were old enough to appreciate—but some of us have the decency to do less talking than thinking. Nettie Coward is fairly mum as a rule, but she can't help showing off to you—wants to impress you with the fact that you've not got a monopoly on all the blood there is. She's a clever woman, but everybody makes an ass of himself one way or another. When we've got twenty generations to the good we'll be just as unconscious about it as you are. But aristocracy will be a sort of itch with us till then. Quantities of idiots have their family trees framed."

I find her very refreshing, Polly.

I have not written much about Mr. N. lately. But I've talked with him!—hours and hours and hours. It is no use trying to avoid him—and he certainly is interesting. Well—heaven knows.

HELEN.

9. P. M.—Your letter has just come. It seems years since I last heard from you. I know how you feel but I can't help being glad that he has gone. Nothing will happen to him. Don't be foolish. He is your manifest destiny and you will be married to him this time next year. If Freddy really has hurt himself and is suffering I can't help feeling sorry for the wicked little beast—I have grown so soft about such things in the last two years. But the circumstances were disgraceful and you were wise to treat his summons to his bedside as a trick to compromise you and hamper the proceedings. What an enigma even a miserable little degenerate can be. Who can say whether he really is fascinated by you still—he is incapable of love—and honestly desires a reconciliation, or whether he wants to prevent your marriage with V. R.—or, who knows?—perhaps he is afraid that woman will want to marry him. Well, I do wish that the evidence could have been gathered more quickly and that it were over.

Letter X

From the Lady HELEN POLE *to the Countess of* EDGE *and* ROSS.

Chipmunk Lake,
August 19th

Dearest Polly:

IT is eleven o'clock P.M., and I have been in bed and asleep since half after seven. I foresee myself wide awake for two hours and giving you an account of the last two days. How flat that sounds—but wait! And otherwise you might never hear of them, for I return to Boulder Lake to-morrow, and in this country events are so quickly crowded into the past.

I wrote you—did I not?—that the subject of a camping expedition had been mooted more than once, but put off from time to time on account of threatening weather and various other causes. I longed to go; "camping out" in the "Adirondack wilderness" being pitched upon a most adventurous and romantic note; and finally I begged Mr. Nugent to arrange it. He went "straight at it" in the energetic American way, and in two hours it was all arranged: Opp drove out in the buckboard for another guide, and Mrs. Opp was making so many good things at once that all the other cooks had to come over to help her. Then Mr. Nugent and Mr. Van Worden packed the big pack-baskets, and everybody was ready to start at nine o'clock the day before yesterday.

The original plan was that all of us should go, but the actual party were Mr. and Mrs. Meredith Jones, Miss Page, Myself, Mr. Nugent, Mr. Latimer, and Mr. Van Worden. The others "backed out" on one excuse or another, and happy it was for them and us that they did.

This colony is only two years old, and, as it happened, none of the men ever had camped out in this part of the Adirondacks before, and as they found their lake and surroundings quite sufficient there was not a tent on the place. However—and the expedition was avowedly got up for my benefit—I insisted that I wanted a genuine rough camping experience, and we all took Opp's word for it that he knew the very spot—where there was fishing, a clearing, and an "open camp," erected by other wood-loving spirits. It is true he grinned as he assured me that I would get a good taste of the "genuine article," but I suspected nothing. What imagination, indeed, would be equal to it!

Mrs. Coward kissed me good-bye quite affectionately, for she expected to "go out" before I returned, and even Mrs. Earle stood on the shore in the little spruce grove and waved her handkerchief with the others as we rowed down the lake.

It was one of those crystal mornings when life seems the divine thing of those imaginings of ours when we have lost for a little the links that hold them to facts. I never felt happier, I was almost excited. It seemed such a delightful thing to float off into the unknown like that, to go in search of adventures, with the certainty that six strong men, one of them your devoted slave, would take the best of care of you. It was all so undiscovered—that rough mountain world beyond the lake—so unimaginable—well, I know all about it now.

We were a very picturesque party, my dear. The men wore white sweaters, corduroy breeches, and top boots. I wore hunter's green, a short skirt of covert cloth just above my boot tops, a linen blouse the same shade and a little bolero to protect my back and arms from the mosquitos. Miss Page, who is very dark, wore a bright red skirt and cap and a red and white striped "shirt waist" with a red tie. Mr. Nugent said she looked exactly like a "stick of peppermint candy," and I am sure I shall recognise that indigestible the first time I enter a "candy store." Mrs. Meredith Jones, who has golden hair and blue eyes, wore a dark blue skirt and cap and the inevitable "shirt waist"; but hers was striped with blue; and the jauntiest little cape hung from her shoulders. Of course we all wore canvas leggins as a further protection from the mosquitoes, which are the least of Adirondack charms.

Well, the moment we stepped on shore our troubles began. We were landed on to a big slippery stone, then handed across several others and a few rotten logs into a swamp. Before us was an impenetrable thicket as high as our heads and wet with dew. We stood staring at it until the guides had shouldered their packs and picked their way over rocks and logs to take the lead.

"That's all right," said Opp, "there ain't bin anyone in here for two years and the road's growed over, but it'll be all right in about a mile. Good trail then. We'll go first and break the road. Wimmin folks'd better bring up in the rear."

So we started; crashing through the wet bushes over the wetter ground until we came to a narrow rocky trail sidling along the inlet. This is a gentle stream in a wild setting. Its rocks are so many and so big that the wonder is the water can crawl over them, and the mountain beside the path is as precipitous as a cliff. None of us paid much attention to the beauties of Nature; we did not dare take our eyes off the path, which had given way in places and was swampy in others. Where it was safe it was rocky. Nor could the men help us much; the trail was too narrow. Single file was a necessity, but Mr. Nugent was just behind me and gave me occasional directions, besides surrounding me, as usual, with an atmosphere of protection. So, slipping, and bending and clutching at trees, we picked our way along until at last the trail turned up hill, and if no less rough was free of the worst element of danger. In another half hour we had passed a lumber camp and were on a level trail along the crest of the mountain. The forest was more open here, so much "lumbering" had been done, but only the spruce were gone—not all of those—and high on one side and down in a valley on the other was the beautiful leafy forest, full of the resinous odor of spruce gum, the spaces rather a welcome change after the forest densities of the last two months. And our procession was very picturesque. The guides with their big pack-baskets strapped to their shoulders were in the lead, almost trotting, that they might outdistance us and have an occasional rest. All our men carried small packs and strode along looking very supple and free, with the exception of poor Mr. Van Worden who is rather stout and must have felt the irksomeness of his pack. But he was enjoying himself, no doubt of that; and indeed, so were we all. Mr. Latimer, who had looked a little conscience-stricken as he said good-bye to

Mrs. Van Worden, whistled as gaily as a schoolboy on a runaway lark. And it was so cool and fresh in the woods, who wouldn't be happy? Not that there was one minute of easy walking—nor an opportunity for sentiment. When we followed the narrow trail through the brush we had to stoop and overlook every inch before we put a foot down. When we were on the long stretches of corduroy, built by the lumbermen to haul their logs over, Mr. Nugent held my hand, but he might have been his ghost for all the impression he made on me, so many were the holes and so rotten some of the logs. Conversation was impossible. We exchanged an occasional remark, but we were all too intent on avoiding sprained ankles and broken tendons—you can not imagine the painfulness of walking too long on log roads—to be interested in any one but ourselves.

There were four hours of this, and good a walker as I am I was beginning to feel tired, when Opp, who had gone far ahead, came in sight again, looking sheepish, rather.

"Be gosh!" he remarked to Mr. Van Worden

as we met, "here's a fine lay out. One of the camps is burned. Them last campers done it, I reckon. I seen 'em go round by way of Spruce Lake."

I heard Mr. Van Worden swear softly under his breath, and saw an expression of blank dismay on Mr. Nugent's face. Mr. Latimer burst into a peal of boyish laughter. But Mr. Meredith Jones said sharply,

"Well let's go on and cook dinner. That is all that concerns us now. We can decide what to do later."

"Are we there?" I asked, hopefully, for I longed to give my poor bruised feet a rest.

"Yes'm," said Opp, "we're there, all right."

And in a moment, Polly, we "were there."

Have you wasted any time, my dear, imagining what an "open camp" is like? I hope not, for it were a waste of good mental energy. The briefest description will fit it. Three sides and a sloping roof, all of bark. The front "open" in the exactest interpretation of the word. Inside—nothing. Twelve feet long and not quite the depth of Mr. Meredith Jones, who is six feet two.

This mansion stood on the edge of a clearing, across which lay a big felled tree. Against this we immediately all sat down in a row. Beyond was a charred ruin and near the log a rude table. Does that sound romantic? I wish you could have seen it. But we all laughed and were happy, and we women, even then, did not realise the true inwardness of the situation. The forest, the beautiful forest, rose on three sides of us; beyond a stream, concealed by alders, was a high sharp ridge of mountains; and we were hungry.

The guides immediately set about making a fire. There seemed to be plenty of logs and they soon had a roaring blaze. Opp found a limb with a forked top, which he drove into the ground just beyond the fire and in the fork transfixed a long curving branch which held a pail of water above the flames. Mr. Nugent and Mr. Van Worden unpacked the baskets, Mr. Meredith Jones set the table, and Mr. Latimer fought off the hornets which swarmed at the first breath of jam and ginger-nuts. When we finally sat about that board, on logs or "any old thing," we eat that excellent luncheon of fried ham and hard boiled eggs, mutton cutlets and fried potatoes, hot chocolate and cake, with a grateful appetite, I can assure you. Mr. Van Worden fried the ham and potatoes and made the chocolate, and we all coddled his culinary pride. All my fatigue vanished, and Mrs. Meredith Jones looked equally fresh and seemed prepared to take whatever might come, with the philosophy of the other sex. But poor Miss Page looked rather knocked up. She has never gone in for walking and her very cap had a dejected air; her fine colour was almost gone, but she looked very pretty and pathetic and all the men attempted to console her.

"I wouldn't mind it," she said with a sigh, "if we didn't have to go back." Then, as if fearing to dampen our spirits with the prospect of carrying her out, she added hopefully, "But it 'll be two days hence. I reckon I'll be all right by that time. I'll just lie about and rest."

When luncheon was over Mr. Latimer made her a comfortable couch of shawls, with a small pack-basket for pillow, and she soon fell asleep.

The guides washed the dishes, then immediately felled two young spruce-trees, and, with the help of Latimer and Mr. Meredith Jones, shaved off the branches and covered the floor of the cabin. This was our bed, my dear, and it was about a foot deep. When it was finished they covered it with carriage robes, and all preparations for nightly comforts were complete. By this time it had dawned on Mrs. Meredith Jones and myself that we were *all* going to sleep under that roof. Opp had examined the sky and predicted rain before morning, and Miss Page was not equal to a return journey—"doubling the road," as they say here—even if any of us had contemplated such a thing.

"Tom and I will sleep in the middle," said Mrs. Meredith Jones reassuringly to me, after an earnest conversation apart with her husband, but I was immensely amused at the whole situation. We were as helpless against certain circumstances as if we did not possess sixpence between us; for it would have taken nearly a day to build another camp and the guides were too tired to think of such a thing. We were all stranded out in space, and there was nothing to do but make the best of it.

About two hours after luncheon I felt as if I had had no exercise that day and Opp suggested that I go up the mountain to see a gorge locally famous. So, accompanied by Mr. N. and Latimer, I followed him up the steepest and roughest mountain of my experience. There was no trail. He trampled ahead through the brush and we followed. Mr. Nugent preceded and literally pulled me up more than one perpendicular place, but Opp insisted upon taking charge of me through the slippery intricacies of a rocky stream. But we were rewarded by the most beautiful spot I have yet seen. Imagine a forest glade with five or six *islands* of rock—boulders so huge that no other word will describe them. These islands were covered on all sides with the richest moss and the most delicate ferns, and on the top of each grew great trees, their long roots gripping the sides of the rock like petrified pythons. Then a water-course choked with smaller boulders, and rising out of it, straight up for five hundred feet, a solid wall of rock crowned with a pine forest. The wall was a half-mile long and so smooth that one could well imagine some terrible convulsion of these Adirondacks during which a mountain had been split in twain, one side grinding itself into these boulder-islands of the forest. On high the tree-tops were so matted that the glade was filled with a twilight almost green. One had the impression of walking under the sea. Each of us selected a dry rock, and we sat there for an hour telling mountain experiences. I had had one or two in the Alps, extremely modest ones, but all the men looked at me with intense admiration as I related them. American men seem to have an almost passionate admiration for women of great physical endurance and courage. Our men take it as a matter of course. Mr. Nugent thought it the most charming thing in the world that I should want "more exercise" after the heavy tramp of the morning. He said one rather clever thing, by the way. The others, after a time, wandered down to the foot of the palisade in search of the ice caves, and as I rather feared that Mr. N., under the influence of the wild beauty about us, might lose a self-control which is plainly manufactured and maintained through a fear of losing everything, (I dread and almost long for the time when it will give way altogether) I turned the conversation to politics and asked him if he looked forward to the possible Bryan administration with the great apprehension that other Republicans seemed to feel.

"No; I can't say I do," he said. "Nothing is ever as bad in politics as the anticipations; anticipations are the exaggerations of much talk. Besides—it is quite on the cards that Bryan will be an arrant snob before he has been a month in the White House. Likely as not, his first taste of Society will induce conservatism. When he has sat at table a few times with titled Ambassadors he will hasten to forget the ridiculous little farm he bought to have his pictures taken in. Then, the only thing left for us to do is to marry his daughter to a gentleman and persuade him to send his son to Harvard. His reform will be accomplished in less than a year. There is no snob so complete as a democrat reformed by the right sort of visiting cards. Of course a small nucleus, the old set of Washington, will not go near the White House, and as soon as the Bryans discover that diplomats, senators, cabinet officers and army people are not all the cream of high society they will become downright aristocrats; and when the shirt-sleeved voter from Lincoln, Nebraska, calls, will conceal their ennui and irritation indifferently well. That means alienation of the sons of the soil, and no second term for Bryan. If Washington is wise it will do its best to make a fool of him."

"You haven't much faith in Mr. Bryan's much vaunted sincerity," I said with a laugh.

"I haven't a particle," he said contemptuously. "He has his picture taken too often."

The others returned at this juncture and we set out upon the difficulties of our homeward journey. But never mind, it was all very delightful and I never shall forget the beauty of that rocky glade.

When we returned to the camp, we found Mrs. Meredith Jones asleep and Miss Page keeping watch. The men had all gone fishing and Mr. Nugent and Mr. Latimer hastened to join them. Miss Page looked refreshed but turned to me a perturbed face.

"I cannot believe it is possible that we are all going to sleep in there," she said. "Why, it is shocking! I begged Mr. Van Worden to put up a partition, but he says it is quite impossible, that there won't be room to turn over, as it is. I wish I hadn't come. Suppose it should get out? Why, people would be horrified."

"Really," I said, "I think you take an exaggerated view. We are all going to bed with our clothes on, the camp is open, there are nine of us, and our chaperons will sleep in the middle. We may not be comfortable but I think the proprieties will take care of themselves."

"I think it is shocking," she said, "perfectly shocking. It seems so coarse and horrid. I'll remember it as long as I live."

I felt like shaking her, but she looked so distressed that I said soothingly: "Please don't worry. I will sleep next to Mrs. Meredith Jones and you can tuck away in the corner where no one can see you and you will be quite forgotten."

"Yes," she replied quickly, "I insist upon having the corner—particularly as you don't mind," she added apologetically. "You are quite different from my idea of English girls. I should have thought that you would be simply horrified."

"Perhaps we are more matter-of-fact than you are," I said drily. "Where a thing can't be helped it can't, and we are sensible about it. Now, I am surprised at you. I had always supposed that American girls——"

"Oh, don't!" she exclaimed. "You are going to judge us all by those horrid things you meet in Europe and in novels. I can assure you that Southern girls—*gentlewomen*—are as particular as English girls—more so, I reckon. Do you realise that we are going to sleep in the same room with six men?"

"I don't look at it in that way at all," I said tartly. "And for heaven's sake make up your mind to the inevitable and think no more about it."

The men returned soon after with a basket full

of trout and Mr. Van Worden fried them for supper. I don't think I ever eat anything quite so good as those trout.

"He beats the cars, cookin,'" observed our chief guide, and Mr. Van Worden looked as pleased as if he had made a million in Wall Street.

After supper the guides built a high fire of great logs, and we all sat about and the men "spun yarns" of the days when the panther and the bear roamed the woods, and finished with stories of the beautiful red deer that alone claims the forest to-day. Of course the men smoked, and we were all very happy and comfortable until we went to bed. Mr. N. sat as close to me as he decently could, and—I will confess to you, Polly—under the encouragement of the shadows which covered a part of me and all of him he held my hand. I could not struggle—well——

About ten the men all marched up the hill in single file, singing, and we had the camp to ourselves for a half hour. We took off our boots, corsets and blouses, put on dressing sacks, tied our heads up in silk handkerchiefs, and our night toilet was complete. Miss Page had evidently made up her mind to accept the situation, but she was so manifestly uncomfortable that I tied nearly all of her face up in her handkerchief and tucked her away in the corner with the blanket up to her nose. She turned her back upon us and regarded the chinks of the bark wall in silent misery. Mr. Van Worden had brought three extra pairs of socks and these he had directed us to pull over our stockings as the night would grow very cold.

We had been in bed nearly twenty minutes and had already learned something of its hardness when the men returned.

"Now," said Opp, "you must all lie on the same side and when one of you wants to turn over be sure to sing out and then we'll all turn over together."

His was the only remark. The other men pulled off their boots and crawled into bed without a word, looking rather sheepish, and ostentatiously refraining from glancing in our direction. Men are certainly more modest than women in certain conditions, and Mrs. Meredith Jones and I almost laughed out loud, especially as the other guide went to bed with his hat on!

For about a half hour we were as quiet as the sardines we must have looked. Then my side—the one I was lying on—began to ache from my neck to my heel, and from the numerous sighs and restless jerks I inferred that we all were affected in the same way. At all events Opp "sang out," "Heave over, hey?" and we all turned like a well-regulated machine. I whispered to Miss Page but she would not answer me.

It was just after that we became conscious that the temperature was about ninety. The fire was not three feet in front of us and blazing more violently every moment. I had been endeavouring to forget my discomfort in watching the black masses of the tree-tops thrown by the blaze into extraordinary relief against the dulled sky and tarnished stars, when I heard Mr. Van Worden whisper fiercely,

"What in heaven's name did you build that

red hot fire for? It's hot enough for three camps and we won't sleep a wink."

Opp replied apologetically: "I thought it was goin' to rain and it was best to have things well het up, but I guess it haint. It's hot and no mistake."

I saw Mr. Latimer fighting to get out of an extra sweater without attracting attention, and I, by the same herculean efforts, managed to reach down and get off my stockings and those socks. But still the heat was insupportable and the bed grew harder every moment. Our pillows, too, were logs under the spruce, and I am used to a baby pillow that I double under my neck and face. How I longed for it!

Finally Latimer slipped out of bed and went over to the edge of the clearing and lit his pipe. The guides followed immediately, then Mr. Meredith Jones, and they sat along the log in dejected silence. Mrs. Meredith Jones heaved a deep sigh. "I really can't stand it, girls," she whispered; and followed her husband. Of course we went too, and Mr. Van Worden was left alone.

For a half hour we sat about in an almost complete silence, waiting for that wretched fire to burn down. Opp separated the logs, and finally, as we were all too sleepy to hold our heads up, we crawled back to bed, one by one, all except Mr. Latimer, who stretched out on the table, and Mr. Nugent who made a bed for himself on the ground. That gave us a trifle more room in the camp, and we could turn without "singing out." In a few minutes, hot as it still was, I fell asleep.

I suppose it was two hours later that I awoke. The fire had taken a fresh start and was blazing more merrily than ever. I felt as if I were in a Turkish bath, and as Miss Page was no longer in front of me I inferred that she had been driven forth again. Then it occurred to me that she would not have budged without Mrs. Meredith Jones, and I turned about quite suddenly. Mrs. M. J. was not there! Nor Mr. M. J. Nor the guides. Oh, Agatha! Agatha! I was alone in bed with Mr. Van Worden.

The situation was humorous, but somewhat

embarrassing. I hardly knew whether to pretend sleep or not, for I did not feel like going out and sitting on that log again. I could see the dark figures in various dejected attitudes. Mrs. M. J. and Miss Page were sitting back to back with their heads hanging, while Mr. M. J. stood with his hands in his pockets glowering at the fire. Latimer was sitting on the table smoking his pipe, and Mr. N. was digging his heels viciously into the earth. As for the guides they lay flat in the distance, tired out, poor things. Only Mr. Van Worden looked serene. He, too, lay on his back, his hands clasped over the greater part of him. I supposed he was asleep, but he remarked genially:

"Hot, isn't it, Lady Helen? I'm afraid one camping experience will do you for the rest of your natural life."

I assured him that I never had been so much entertained, and we conversed as naturally as if it had been noon-day until I was reminded of the irregularities of the situation by a gasp from Miss Page. She nudged Mrs. M. J., whispered hurriedly, and in another moment I was chaperoned on either side.

It was at least another hour before the fire burned down and the temperature cooled. Then the men crawled back to bed, one by one, and in a few moments they were all sleeping—and as quietly as kittens. It really was quite remarkable.

But one could not sleep long at a time on that bed, and once I was glad to be awake. High up on the highest tree of the mountain a hoot owl broke the petrified stillness of that lonely forest.

"Too wit, too wit, too wooo!" he called loudly, and then he added with impatient emphasis, "Too wit, too wit, *too woo*," as if to say, "Do you understand that?" He was a bit of a scold, but he had all the grey dome and all the forest depths to talk into. No comrade answered him, and nothing ever gave me such an impression of the solitude of a mountain forest,

By six o'clock we had endured all that the human frame is capable of in the way of sleeping on hard and prickly spruce, and the men rose as by one impulse and went down to the spring to wash. We dressed as hurriedly as possible, and, I must say, looked surprisingly fresh. And the morning was so deliciously cool, and Mr. Van Worden's coffee so fragrant and bracing, his trout so crisp and Mrs. Opp's "johnnie cake," so excellent that we sat about Mr. Latimer's bed in the highest spirits and congratulated each other that we were "camping out." Even Miss Page, having weathered the worst of it, announced herself ready to stay another night, and talked continually in her pretty Southern brogue. She was looking like a beautiful gypsy, too, and I think our one small mirror had consoled her for many things. She flashed her eyes about with the impartiality of the kind-hearted coquette, and was quite the life of the uncomfortable group about the table.

After breakfast Mrs. M. J., Latimer, Mr. Nugent and myself, led by Opp, with an axe over his shoulder, started off to see some famous falls. The rest went fishing. As the trail along the "still-water" had been choked by lumbermen, Opp had to rely on his general knowledge of the land, and every few minutes he "blazed" a tree, *i.e.*, hacked off a piece of the bark with his axe, that there should be no danger of going astray when we returned. The ground was less broken up than usual and we strode along in single file looking for all the world like a party of pioneers penetrating the wilderness. It was a jolly experience and I would not have missed it for anything.

The falls were about two miles from the camp and we were an hour reaching them, for Opp got off the track several times. I can imagine that they look very fine indeed when there is anything falling. But all we saw was a sloping wall of solid rock, about four hundred and fifty feet high and a fifth of a mile wide, crowned with spruce. There is a deep wide pool below, and a mass of rocks on which we sat and tried to picture the mighty cascade of other seasons. On one end—the perpendicular end—of the wall there were soil and trees, and Opp asked me if I would like to "climb the falls and see the sights." I was half way across the rocks in a moment with Mr. N. and Latimer after me, while Opp remained with Mrs. M. J.

It was a straight climb, my dear, of four

hundred and fifty feet. It hardly sloped once and there was just one ledge of about six steps. We had to pull ourselves up by trees and bushes, and more that once Mr. N. dragged me up, while Mr. L. pushed me. But altogether I did rather well, and was quite rewarded by their enthusiastic approval. But there was a better reward than that. From an elevation above the falls we saw five mountain ranges. They seemed to fill all space, and the blue dome to press down its rim about them, holding such a flood of crystal and gold! There were many beautiful pines about us, sage green with a delicate fairy-like quality in spite of their greatness, and once more the undesecrated forest, so dense that Mr. N. had noted every inch of ground we traversed.

Of course it was worse going down than ascending and I was glad to have two men to take care of me.

Well, we spent all of that day very pleasantly, and the night promised to be rather more comfortable, for Mr. Nugent, Mr. Latimer, and the guides all made beds for themselves under the stars and the fire was left to go out after supper. But, alas! about midnight it began to rain, they all came crawling under shelter, and there was little more sleep that night.

The rain stopped long enough for us to breakfast comfortably, and then we held a consultation. The plan had been to "stay out" three nights, but we were all a little tired of it, and the skies looked very forbidding.

"If you want my opinion," remarked Opp, "I say go, and be quick about it. It's set in for all day, and if we git back to the Lake without a soakin' we'll be luckier 'n I think we will."

That settled it. We had no desire to sit on our bed all day and then sleep on it another night. The guides began to pack at once, and within an hour we were on our way.

We had hardly started when it began to pour, and it has not stopped yet. What a walk it was! However we reached home without pneumonia and broken ankles heaven only knows, but not one of us has a cold; and although my feet feel as if they had been pounded with a hammer they are quite whole. When we were not picking our way over the narrow trail through the brush—dripping and as high as our heads—we were on those horrible corduroy roads, made so slippery by the rain that every step was a danger. Once I fell, and I twisted my foot three times and wrenched myself up to my waist. My feet were swimming in my boots and it was an effort to lift them. I felt sorry for Miss Page, who is a pampered creature, but she never uttered a complaint, although she told me afterward that every time we came to one of those interminable stretches of corduroy she wanted to sit down and cry. She certainly is a fine creature, with all her little foibles.

When we got to the lumber camp we all sat down in the rain and rested before climbing the corduroy hill beyond. Mr. N. explained to me the use of the curious objects piled under a shed. They were huge boxes on runners with four round holes in each end. When the snow is on the ground, covering corduroy and rocks, these boxes are filled with water and dragged by horses over the road to be used for drawing the lumber to the streams. From the front holes the water spouts continuously, and as it strikes the ground it freezes, making a solid smooth surface over which the log sledges can travel with ease. But what a life! No wonder these mountaineers look old; but Mr. N. told me that lumbermen become so fascinated with the life that they cannot be tempted into the valleys.

You can imagine the difficulties of that narrow sidling swampy trail by the inlet. It was just twice as bad as in dry weather, and I almost was discouraged once or twice. Perhaps I should have been, had it not been for a very reassuring and helpful presence; but it was bad enough.

Latimer had hastened on to the lake to fire his revolver, the signal that we were coming. When the rest of us arrived the boats were almost there, but as we were all hot and wet, and a cold wind played upon us as we stood on the stones again, it is a wonder we are not all wrecks. As soon as I reached home Mrs. Van Worden made me drink hot whiskey, while Mrs. Opp and Henriette undressed and rubbed me down. I am none the worse for wear, but felt quite done up by half-after seven and went to bed. Hence this great letter. Good night. I return to Boulder Lake to-morrow.

HELEN

Boulder Lake
August 20th
10 P.M.

I forgot to give this letter to the postman to-night so I will tell you of two or three surprises which have made me wide-awake, rather.

Of course Mr. Nugent returned with me, (and as there is always a room at the Club House at his disposal I suppose he will remain through the deer and grouse seasons—unless—but I vow I don't know!) I was glad to see that beautiful avenue dividing the dark forest, once more, and we walked slowly, the buckboard following. I can't say the familiar corduroy filled me with sentimental emotions and my insteps ached at the first glimpse of it; but I have that buoyancy within that carries my feet over many a weary mile, and my companion, as ever, was very interesting. I forget just what we talked about.

We were half way up the last hard bit of corduroy and my eyes as usual were intent upon the logs when Mr. N. said abruptly:

"Look!"

I stopped at once and followed the direction of his glance. Before I had time to wonder if he had seen a bear I saw, standing on the ledge above, Mr. Rogers—and Bertie! The light was full upon them and I saw in a flash that Bertie was stouter and had lost his terrible pallor. He was not ruddy, but he was brown, and there was colour in his cheeks.

Polly, did you ever have a wild whirl of emotions inside of you while you forced your exterior to be as impassive as a shell? I wanted to give one of the war-whoops with which they call to one another up here, and I felt so much like bursting into a storm of tears that I dared not even speak.

When Bertie and I met we merely shook hands, and he remarked that he was glad to see me back, but I knew he wanted to hug me. Then I gave my hand to Mr. Rogers—and was just in time to see the look with which my two knights were measuring each other.

I walked ahead with Bertie and he said that between the air and the milk he certainly was getting well, and I found my voice and told him that I never had felt so happy in my life. But my absorption in Bertie was divided for the moment by a new surprise.

We had left the level stretch and were walking down the incline to the boat landing (I had been too interested to notice that we had not turned off into the path leading to our camp), when I stopped short with half a sentence forgotten. Waiting at the pier was a gondola—a gondola with silken curtains and cushions and an Italian gondolier.

Bertie laughed gaily at my startled face, for in truth I was afraid for the moment that something in my brain had gone wrong.

"Rogers sent for it—to Chicago, of all places!" he said. "It is a remnant of the World's Fair."

And then I remembered I once had said to Mr. Rogers that I could not understand why they did not have gondolas on these beautiful lakes instead of commonplace boats.

All my coquetry was enchanted and I turned to Mr. Rogers with such a radiant face that he must have felt a bit rewarded. While I was thanking him—glad of that much outlet for my excitement—and he was making one of his charming speeches and looking so dignified and not the least bit of an ass, I stole a glance at Mr. N. His face wore a cynical grin that was almost sardonic.

Well, I gondolaed home and fell into Agatha's arms, then discovered Bertie's welcome. He had —himself, mind you—tacked that most beautiful of shrubs, the ground pine, all over the walls of the living room. They looked a mass of soft green and gold and the antlered heads of the deer seemed to be set in their native woods. On the table was a great bunch of crimson sweet peas—incomparably more fragrant than ours—sent by Jemima, and a bowl of water lilies from Mrs. Laurence.

After I had answered all of Agatha's questions and assured her that I was as well as ever—she thinks I am thin, but how I have tramped!—Bertie and I went out and gondolaed round the lake. It was just five o'clock. The men were going home from the tennis court, and waved their hats at me and gave the unearthly wood call.

Then, suddenly, all the doors opened, and the women in their bright muslin gowns flitted out and waved their handkerchiefs to me. It was a pretty sight and a graceful act. Of course, I landed and they said a great many of their charming things.

When I went home another surprise awaited me—in my room. On the table was a box of splendid roses and an elaborate basket of chocolates tied with yards of my favourite bright blue ribbon. Mr. Nugent's card was attached. Of course he had sent to New York for them.

I don't think I ever went to bed feeling so happy.

HELEN

21st

I suppose we have all taken note of that malignant influence in the unseen world which makes us unreasoningly and unguardedly happy just before our stiffest blows. One would think these bitter contrasts were purposely arranged to destroy our power of philosophy.

It was at breakfast that I was confounded, more nearly knocked over than I ever was in my life.

"By the way, Nell," Bertie remarked casually, "what a ripping fine woman Mrs. Coward is?"

"Mrs. Coward?" I gasped.

"Yes. Don't mean to say you didn't know she was here?"

"I did not!" I could barely articulate. And a perturbed glance from Agatha increased my consternation. "When did she come?"

"Three or four days ago—Oh, yes, she said you had left the same morning for your camping tramp."

"Whom is she visiting? I had no idea the aristocracies would mix."

"Mrs. Laurence. Don't you like Mrs. Coward?"

"I am glad she is visiting Mrs. Laurence. I should say they would scratch each other's eyes out immediately."

"I'm disappointed you don't like her. I hoped you'd have her in the house a lot. She's a long sight the most fascinating American I ever met—a regular ripper, by gad!"

I don't know how I controlled myself, but I knew that if I said too much and suggested opposition Bertie would be on his hind legs at once.

This was what she had up her sleeve, Polly. What deceit, what treachery, what sneakingness. Only a *widow* would be capable of such a thing. But I must say I respect her. She fooled me completely. I could not have been capable of so clever a revenge, and I detest her for it, because she has not the true sporting instinct, but she is to be reckoned with all the same. In spite of her platitudes and her ingenuous pride in the seven generations, she is both clever and deep—when her pride is in arms, and revenge and ambition both spur her on to capture a duke.

But *will* she marry him? *Oh!* Many moths have

fluttered about that flame. But she is so subtle. And in addition to her indisputable magnetism she has developed fascination into a fine art. Of course she has scented out all Bertie's weak points and flattered them. I can hear her discoursing about the solemn responsibilities of the hereditary legislator, and that is what is haunting Bertie most at present. Of course she knows all about Dad, and her dulcet enthusiasms on that convenient weakness—Oh, *dear!* Agatha says they have been almost inseparable since the afternoon she arrived. She did not lose a minute!

He actually asked me if he could take her out in *my gondola*. I felt like telling him to take her out and drown her, but I gave my consent as graciously as I could, and came into the house to think. I dare not go to the forest, for I know that Mr. N. is lying in wait for me and I feel certain that after this gondola declaration he will press his suit; and when he *does* plant himself on both feet in the middle of the trail and I on the wrong side—Oh, heaven!

I induced Agatha to go over to the tennis court

so that I could not receive Mr. Rogers if he called. But for some time I could not even write to you, I could only storm up and down the living-room and try to think of some way to foil that woman and deliver Bertie. Fancy having her for a sister-in-law! And she would radiate a subtle triumph till the day of her death. But the real—underlying—point is that she is not the wife for Bertie. He must marry an intelligent woman who will give herself to him and his career, and this one would be entirely wrapped in her own petty ambitions.

It suddenly occurred to me that Miss Page had promised to spend the first two weeks of September with me. She is still at Chipmunk Lake, for the other women do not leave for two days yet. The buckboard had not gone. I wrote her a note, imploring her to come at once as I was bored and lonely. Then I bribed the driver to take it to her to-day, and he said he would wait and bring her back. She is far more beautiful than Mrs. C., and younger. She may not be so subtle but she has all the fascination of a buoyant and unaffected coquette. And she is worth six of Mrs. C. as regards character and sincerity. Not, alas! that that adds to one's power over man. But I am hoping that Bertie will contrast her real brightness with Mrs. C.'s platitudes, and discover that the widow is boring, that he will succumb to Miss Page's superior beauty, and that propinquity will do its work. If only it doesn't all happen before she gets here! Mrs. C. has had him in her pocket for three hours—*in my gondola.* She has on a white frock and a scarlet shawl and a red poppy in her hair. There is no denying that she is hideously attractive. Oh, Polly, how I wish you were here!

To add to my burdens Bertie gave me, this morning—he mercifully forgot it last night—an impassioned epistle from Mr. Carlisle. His mother is better and he is returning to Chipmunk Lake for the hunting season. He says he shall devote three days a week to deer and the rest to me—that if they won't invite him to the Club House he'll camp on the next lake, which is only a mile away and on State lands. But of course they'll invite him to the Club House. Oh, Polly! Do you think any woman ever was in such a tangle before!

On the whole I think I'll go out into the forest and talk to Mr. N. about it. I *must* talk to somebody or I'll have brain fever. And I'm used to diverting his mind—"standing him off," as they say here. And I want sympathy.

This is really good-bye. I won't write another line till I am in a more cheerful state of mind—induced by Miss Page's triumph over the widow—for I do not want to add to your worries.

HELEN

P.S.—Roddy Spencer will arrive on one of the Saturday steamers.

NOTE.—*The correspondence ends abruptly with the above letter; Lady Helen Pole, on the following day having received a cablegram announcing the sudden death of the Earl of Edge and Ross and the immediate departure of her friend for the United States.*

THE PUBLISHER.

THE END.